TASTING
LIGHT

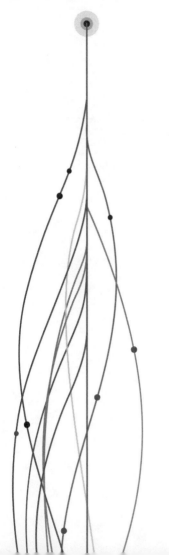

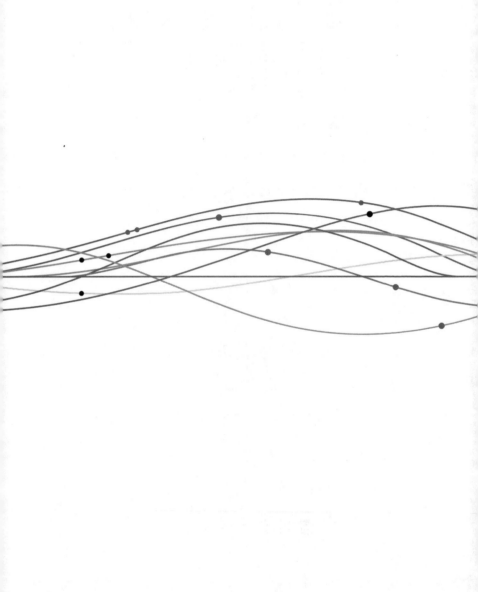

TASTING LIGHT

LIGHT

TEN SCIENCE FICTION STORIES TO REWIRE YOUR PERCEPTIONS

EDITED BY

A. R. CAPETTA

AND

WADE ROUSH

Compilation copyright © 2022 by A. R. Capetta and Wade Roush
"Cadence" copyright © 2022 by Charlotte Nicole Davis
"On the Tip of My Tongue" copyright © 2022 by William Alexander
"Melanitis" copyright © 2022 by Junauda Petrus-Nasah
"Extremophiles" copyright © 2022 by A. R. Capetta
"The Memory of Soil" copyright © 2022 by Wendy Xu
"Walk 153" copyright © 2022 by K. Ancrum
"The Weight of a Name" copyright © 2022 by Nasuġraq Rainey Hopson
"Twin Strangers" copyright © 2022 by Elizabeth Bear
"The Cage" copyright © 2022 by E.C. Myers
"Smile River" copyright © 2022 by A.S. King

The MIT Press, the ≡MiTeenPress colophon, and MITeen Press are trademarks of The MIT Press, a department of the Massachusetts Institute of Technology, and used under license from The MIT Press. The colophon and MITeen are registered in the US Patent and Trademark Office.

First edition 2022

Library of Congress Catalog Card Number 2021953326
ISBN 978-1-5362-1938-8

22 23 24 25 26 27 LBM 10 9 8 7 6 5 4 3 2 1

Printed in Melrose Park, IL, USA

This book was typeset in Minion Pro.
The illustrations in "The Memory of Soil" were created digitally in Procreate.

MITeen Press
an imprint of Candlewick Press
99 Dover Street
Somerville, Massachusetts 02144

miteenpress.com
candlewick.com

CONTENTS

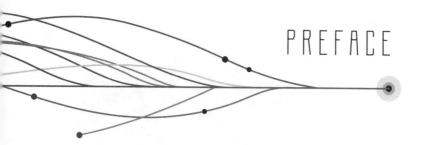

Hey, Wade!

Good morning, A. R.! How are you? Let's do this!

I'm ready! Let's go!

It's been so fun working with you on this project for, what, the last year and a half? I can't believe we're almost finished. I'll miss swimming in all these wonderful words.

I wish we could do a quick time travel flyby to tell our past selves that the stories would be so amazing.

It's also funny/wild to think that we didn't know each other or talk all the time a year ago.

And that we still haven't met in person! We'll look back on that as one of the many weird things about the pandemic. Speaking of which, the pandemic does make a cameo in the book (we'll let readers figure out where). But all of these stories are set in the future, because that's what our writers gravitated toward. What I'm particularly happy about is how they all found ways to write classic YA fiction—stories about young people discovering themselves and how their bravery can change the world in small or big ways—but do it within the bounds of hard science fiction. Meaning no magic, no faster-than-light travel, just real-world physics. We gave them a puzzle, and they solved it brilliantly.

Yes! I love how each writer took on the human relationship to science. And everyone wrote in a way that doesn't ignore actual teenagers. They're so likely to be the ones interacting first with new tech, insisting on new ideas, imagining a way forward. And yet we so often still see science portrayed as a thing that only specific adults do. In lab coats.

So true! I started off thinking the main point of this anthology would be to introduce more young readers to hard science fiction. In the end, I think this collection of stories accomplishes something else, too: stretching the boundaries of YA SF a bit to show that it's a perfect genre for examining the issues of identity that young people have always grappled with, but which have moved closer to the center of our cultural conversation today.

Feels so important to me to have fewer boundaries in SF. And more open space to explore. (Sometimes literally.)

When you have expansive ideas around what a SF story can be, you're not limiting the ways people can imagine the future or illuminate the present.

SF should be a field of so many possibilities and perspectives. And that's what I feel excited and, really, honored to share with this collection.

Me too! People who know I've been working on this project have been asking if this book has a theme. The fact is that these stories cover such a vast array of settings and times and technologies that there's really no central topic. But maybe there's a central *feeling*—that the future is going to be better than the present, as long as we try to make it that way. To me, that's the core of good futurism. Our writers have taken our reality, vaulted a bit into the future, and added twists like sentient robots and voice transplants and parallel dimensions (maybe?) and aliens under the ice of Europa (maybe?) to see what might happen. Those propositions are all cool and provocative on their own. But what I really love is the way our writers have used them in the service of stories that are ultimately about identity. Who gets to explore? Who gets to love and be loved? Can we learn from our mistakes? Who can save the day?

How can we be true to our deepest selves? How can we interact with people—with the universe itself—in a different way? That last one relates to the title . . . which we didn't know if we would ever find! And then in the end, it was right in front of us, like an emergent property of the stories as a whole.

Yeah, that part was real magic. I know people are going to ask us what the title means, and we can't say much without spoilers. But there's a clear suggestion of synesthesia and unexpected sensor readings—moments when you're knocked off-kilter just enough to make you adjust your sense of what's possible. Which is what good SF is about, right?

Right. A shift or spark in perception that allows us to understand reality in a whole new light. (Pun . . . kind of intended.)

So, to the readers who've picked up this book with open minds and senses, it's time to go forth into what we're all here for—the stories!

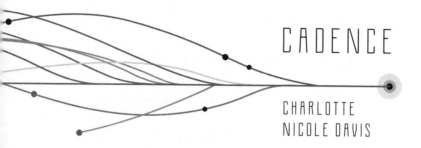

CADENCE

CHARLOTTE NICOLE DAVIS

S O M E voices are copyrighted. You can't be Beyoncé. But, for enough money, you can be just about anyone else.

Cadence has been saving up for this. They have been taking extra shifts at Scoops, the soles of their shoes *rip-rip-ripping* across the sticky floor as they scurry around behind the counter, serving ice cream to rich suburban kids with forked tongues and slitted pupils. Cold-blooded, primeval: this is the look. Wymie Park sent his models down the runway with serpent mods last spring, and now everybody who's anybody is wearing them.

Cadence is not anybody. Cadence is just another teenage twink-dyke tripping over the dirty gray laces of their Converse sneakers. There is a scribble where their brain should be. But they need a new speaking voice, they are confident of this much, at least. They are not chasing a trend, they are righting a wrong.

No one seems to understand this.

If you're going to drop all that money on a mod, at least get a good *one,* Cadence's older brother said. *Your voice is fine. Fix your face.*

Everybody hates the sound of their own voice, honey, Cadence's mother said. *You can't just mod your way out of every little insecurity. You have to learn to love yourself as you are.*

No, Cadence's father said.

And so Cadence made their appointment in secret and went to the mod center alone, and now here they are, preparing to listen to the voices of the dead.

"Do you have a preference for the age, gender, or accent of your donor?" the woman in white asks. She wears a lab coat like a doctor's and holds a tablet. Her red-painted nails look as hard and shiny as the backs of beetles.

"Um," Cadence says blankly. They have thought long and hard about all of this, of course, but now that the moment is here at last, they can barely remember their own name. It is too bright in here, and too hard, and too cold, all white glass and gleaming steel, like a hospital or an Apple Store.

The woman, who has some kind of derma-mod that makes her white skin glitter faintly, presses on. "Some of our most popular accents for English speakers are Southern American English, Eastern New England English, and Received Pronunciation, or 'the Queen's English.' Our donors range in age from thirteen to eighty-seven years old, men and women both. Unless you want to take a look at our selection of custom voices, of course?"

That "men and women both" does not go unnoticed, but

Cadence tries to ignore it and focus on the question being asked. The custom voices are the nonhuman ones, the cyborg warbles, the reptilian rasps. But Cadence wants to sound human, and that can only be achieved by borrowing another human's voice. These are harvested from willing donors, like organs, digitally scanned and reproduced while the donor is still alive. It's only once the donor is deceased that their voice can be used—taking on the voice of another living person risks interfering with voice recognition technology and the security it provides.

It is safe enough, though, to accept a gift from the dead.

Cadence is tempted to use this voice to take on a new personality entirely. A slurring surfer from California, a posh British exchange student, a crabby old grandparent asking after their iced tea. But that is not the point of this. At the end of the day, Cadence just wants to sound like themself: a mild-mannered kid from Missouri.

"If I get a teenager's voice, will I sound like a teenager forever?" Cadence asks, finally finding words. They are eighteen and almost out of these particular woods. They do not want their voice to hold them back.

"No—without intervention, your new voice will age naturally. But we can do a follow-up in a few years to address that, if you want."

That won't be necessary. Cadence is excited for their new voice to grow and change with them, to become worn and comfortable. It is this first part they are worried about, when it will pinch like new shoes. All of high school has felt like that. Who would want that forever?

"I want a young adult voice, then, please, with a Midwestern accent. The gender doesn't matter," Cadence says, because it will not be a boy's or a girl's voice once it is in their mouth.

The woman presses her thin lips together. Cadence begins to sweat, shifting uncomfortably in the hard plastic chair. They know that there are unspoken rules to body modification, that you can become a different type of boy or girl as long as you *remain* either a boy or a girl. Cadence has a cousin who had her skin lightened, shares a locker with a white boy weeb who gave himself anime eyes. These things are allowed. But the modification industry has been careful to distance itself from "fringe" cultures that "abuse" the technology—and in this part of the world in particular, they are more conservative still. Legally, they cannot deny Cadence gender-affirming services. But they can wrinkle their nose at the idea.

"Right this way, then," the woman says after a moment.

Cadence is suddenly very lonely. Their eyes burn with the threat of tears as they follow the woman to the sound booth. They wonder if they are doing the right thing. They wonder if it will hurt. But once they start listening to the voices, they begin to feel a little bit better. Excited, even. They have waited years for this. They will savor the moment.

The first voice belongs—belonged—to a nineteen-year-old from Chicago named Marcus Tomlin. His voice is deep, deeper than Cadence's natural speaking voice, with a flat accent that's a little stronger than Cadence is looking for. "He thrusts his fists against the posts and still insists he sees the ghosts," he says. This is probably not something Marcus ever said in life. It is just a sample sentence, one that shows off the capabilities of the computer-generated re-creation. He says more things, like "The jolly collie swallowed a lollipop" and "Lesser leather never weathered wetter weather better." It is a bold, brassy speaking voice. It exudes confidence, control. Cadence would like, desperately, to be that kind of person. But it would be the wrong reason to choose a voice. Confidence is not something you can just graft onto yourself; Cadence's mother was right about that much. The confidence will come from having chosen the *right* voice, not from the voice itself.

They move on.

The next voice belonged to a fifteen-year-old from Ohio named Chris Li. His voice is higher, lighter, and it has a ringing quality to it, like it's constantly on the edge of laughter. Something about this fills Cadence with an acute sadness. All the voices they will hear are from young donors, but fifteen is *very* young. They wonder how Chris died. They wonder if, when Chris got his parents to sign off on him being a donor, he had any idea he'd be taken so soon. And they wonder why he even became a donor in the first place. There is money in it—not much, but enough to make a difference for many people. For others, it's about immortality. But for someone as young as Chris, it was probably for the status. If you can't afford your own mods, saying you've donated one is the next best thing. Whatever the reason, Cadence cannot shake the feeling that they would be stealing something from Chris by choosing this mod—or maybe, more accurately, taking something that was stolen. And they cannot bear the weight of that.

They move on.

An hour passes. Two. Cadence can tell the woman in white is getting annoyed. If Cadence doesn't pick a voice soon, they will have to reschedule the whole procedure. They do not know if they will find the courage a second time.

Maybe this is a sign. Maybe this is not meant to be.

"This next one strays outside your preferred regional accent, but we're running out of options," the woman says, somewhat stiffly. She taps on her tablet and pulls up the next profile. This one belonged to an eighteen-year-old from Dallas named Reina Pérez. "He thrusts his fists against the post and still insists he sees the ghost," she says, like all the others. And the woman is right: this voice is not *quite* newscaster neutral. There is a taste of Texas here. But that is not what catches Cadence's ear. It is the soft lull of it, low and deep, warm and strong, like sunlight, if it had a sound. There is a natural musicality to it, too. It would have been a good singing voice. It might still be. Cadence tries to picture the person it once belonged to, but instead, they see themself.

This is the one. Cadence knows immediately. They get the same feeling of rightness in their chest as when they changed their hair for the first time, or when they started wearing clothes from the other side of the department store. All day, they have been smiling fake smiles for others' sake and not their own, but the smile spreading across their face now is real.

"I think that's it," they say quietly.

The woman seems almost as relieved as Cadence to be at the end of their search. She escorts them to an operating room, though it's not actually called that—that would be too off-putting. Instead, it is a "reinvention room." There's soft music piping in and a television on mute, perhaps to distract from the fact that the countertops are covered with sharp, gleaming tools. There is a large contraption like a dentist's chair in the middle of the room, made of gray-blue leather, like the back of a whale. Much like a dental cleaning, this procedure won't take more than half an hour.

Cadence is beginning to feel afraid again. Now they are truly alone—even the woman in white has left, on to her next client. There is no one here to hold their hand. They climb into the dentist's chair, lean back, stare up into the harsh white lights. Their throat catches when they swallow. It is such a vulnerable part of the body, they think. Cut the throat, and life pours out.

This time, though, life will pour in. They will wake new and whole.

The door opens, and three nurses swarm in, their faces covered by goggles and soft blue surgical masks. They prep Cadence for the procedure.

"Any last words?" one of them asks jokingly. Then she sees the terrified look on Cadence's face and tries to take it back. "Oh, honey, I'm sorry—it was a joke. Because you're getting your voice replaced. I didn't mean . . ."

"Oh," Cadence says.

"Everything's going to be just fine, I promise. This your first mod?"

Cadence nods. Their head is beginning to swim, and they don't know if it's from the fear pumping through their blood or the sedative.

"Just count backward from one hundred, Cadence," the nurse says. "You'll be on the other side of this before you know it."

One hundred, ninety-nine, ninety-eight, ninety-seven . . .

"Cadence? Cadence, it's Dr. Chase. You're in the recovery room. How are you feeling? Easy, now, your throat's going to be a little sore. Just a thumbs-up or thumbs-down will do. Perfect. Now, open your mouth for me, let's have a look. Great—it's healing up great. You did a great job, Cadence. I'm writing you a prescription for some hydrocodone for the pain. You're going to want to rest your voice completely for the next forty-eight hours and continue to treat it gently for the next four to six weeks: no whispering, no shouting, no singing, no prolonged conversations. It's all written down on your discharge form. But before I go, I do want to hear you try and say something, just to make sure everything's sounding right. Go on, now—it can be anything. 'Mary had a little lamb.' "

Cadence's brain is still heavy with fog. They barely remember what words are. And yet, suddenly, there are some forming on the tip of their still-numb tongue.

"Ask me again tomorrow," they say—and at the sound of their new voice, they weep with joy.

Aaliyah has come to the park to get away.

In fact, Aaliyah has moved her entire life to the great state of Missouri to get away. She is staying with her grandmother, sleeping on the floral-printed guest bed, finishing up high school five hundred miles away from where she started it. It is not far enough: the grief has followed her. She feels it crowding in on her in the already-cluttered living room, where the coffee table is piled high with loose-leaf homework assignments and old cereal bowls crusted with milk and little orange pill bottles filled with antidepressants. The blinds have been opened to let the white winter sunlight in, and her grandmother has the Luther Vandross Christmas album playing through the house, but none of it is enough to chase away the shadows that close in whenever Aaliyah sits still for too long.

And so she has come to the park to get away from her getaway, even though it is colder than a witch's tit out here, as her grandmother would say.

She is not the only one here. It's a Saturday afternoon, and there's still snow on the ground from earlier in the week. Kids are sledding down the big hill until it's bald with dirt, ducking out from behind dead trees to throw snowballs at each other. There's an ice-skating rink, too, and a cart that sells apple cider and hot chocolate, and a towering Christmas tree strung with colored lights and ornaments as big as a grown man's head. Aaliyah is careful, as she walks the path that winds through the park, not to slip on the patches of ice or step in the frigid puddles of melted snow. She's not wearing snow boots, doesn't own any, never needed them before now.

All of this hurts to see: the little kids playing hard with their best friends, the couples clinging to each other on the skating rink, and the snow, which Reina had loved so much but never got to see like this. Aaliyah doesn't know why she thought it would be a good idea to come here. She feels hollowed out, rotten. She belongs somewhere dark and quiet, not here in all this hard, glittering brightness, this celebration, this noise. She resents these people for their happiness. It is offensive. It is not right that they should be here when Reina is not.

Aaliyah lets out a heavy breath that frosts in the air. She is about to turn around and go home.

It is then that she hears Reina's voice.

"Should auld acquaintance be forgot, and never brought to mind . . ."

Aaliyah stops cold. At first, she assumes it is someone else's voice, that, in her sorrow, she is hearing Reina in every minor key. But no—that is her. Aaliyah would recognize her voice anywhere. She has heard it almost every day of her life since she was eight years old.

Aaliyah is suspended, weightless, the ground suddenly gone beneath her.

She begins to run.

"Watch it," a man growls when Aaliyah shoves past him. She does not stop to apologize, even as she plows through another knot of people. She does not slow down, even as her shoes slip on the slick pavement. She is getting closer. She is almost there. She can hear Reina's voice, high and clear on the wind.

"Should auld acquaintance be forgot, and days of auld lang syne?"

Aaliyah reaches the quad where the Christmas tree is set up. There is a kid about her age sitting at its base, a beat-up black guitar in their lap. They are long and lanky, like a bundle of crazy straws, and brown-skinned, with snowflakes caught in their twists. Their fingers move quickly over the frets. The guitar case is at their feet, its red mouth open for tips. The kid is singing.

They are singing with Reina's voice.

Aaliyah has slowed to a walk, but she cannot stop herself from approaching. One foot falls in front of the other, inexorably. It is as if she's in a trance.

It's . . . a mod, Aaliyah realizes as the singing continues.

She doesn't know what she expected to find. Reina, alive somehow? Her ghost, in a park in the middle of Missouri? She hates that she hoped for these things, even for an instant. But the truth feels even more absurd somehow.

A fucking mod?

Aaliyah has seen plenty of mods today. Moms with neon lights underneath their nails, flashing red and green for the holiday. Dads with reindeer antlers or elf ears. Aaliyah's grandmother would have had a thing or two to say about all that. She does not care for mods under any circumstance—she thinks people are tampering with the Lord's will, defiling the temple of the body—but she would find these particularly crass. "Keep the Christ in Christmas," she is always saying.

Aaliyah does not share her grandmother's ill will toward mods. In fact, she hopes to be covered with them one day, as soon as she's free of this place. But in this moment, hearing Reina's voice coming out of this stranger's mouth, as if they've consumed her somehow, Aaliyah is filled with sudden revulsion.

She closes the remaining distance between them and snatches the guitar away, throttling it by its neck. It lets out a strangled yelp. The kid flinches back and looks up at her owlishly.

"What the hell do you think you're doing?" Aaliyah demands.

"I'm . . . singing Christmas carols? Do I need a license to do that in this part of the park or something?"

Aaliyah does not know if she can bear this. Hot tears are pouring down her face, burning in the cold.

"I mean your *voice*. That's not your *voice*," Aaliyah says finally.

Aaliyah has gotten the impression that this kid doesn't know how to fight, but something in their face hardens at this accusation. They jump up and snatch their guitar back.

"Yes, it is."

"No, it's *not*," Aaliyah half sobs. "I knew the girl it belonged to. Her name was Reina Pérez. We grew up together. And you have no right to—no right to—"

"Is everything all right here?" a concerned citizen huffs, walking up to them. He has a Captain America jawline that is clearly a mod and a generally racist air about him. He does not appreciate these two Black kids getting loud in his park. Aaliyah swallows and locks eyes with the kid through her tears. They look scared again.

"It's fine. We were just leaving," she sighs.

The man lingers while Aaliyah helps the kid pack up their stuff, and they walk off together in silence. The kid chews their lip. They do not look at Aaliyah.

"I'm sorry," they mumble finally. "I mean, I'm sorry for your loss. Your friend, she . . . she saved my life."

Aaliyah does not know what to say to that. What does it matter that this stranger's life was saved if the cost was Reina's?

"Do you want to—can we go to a coffee shop or something?" they continue. "I need to get something hot for my throat. My voice is still kind of—anyway, I just feel like maybe we should talk about this. My name's Cadence, by the way."

Aaliyah does not offer her name in return. She doesn't want to go to a coffee shop. She doesn't want to go home, either. There is nowhere on this earth she wants to be right now.

But she does want to—need to—keep hearing Reina's voice. It hurts to hear, yes, but the silence has been more agonizing still.

She nods once. "What's close to here?"

Cadence takes her to a little place nearby. It is bright, frothy, and pink. Aaliyah hates it on sight. The rush of warm air ought to be a relief after so long in the cold, but instead it is muggy and suffocating, the constant noise unbearably loud in such a small space. Cadence seems equally overwhelmed, looking a little like a lost child.

This was a mistake.

"Let me buy you something," Cadence says tentatively.

"I've got it," Aaliyah says, cutting them off. She plunges into the crowd that surrounds the counter and orders a black coffee to match her mood. Cadence follows, but she leaves them to fend for themself, retreating to find a table. There is an empty one near the front window. It is tiny, not much bigger than a dinner plate, and the chairs are equally, ridiculously, twee. She squeezes into one and waits stonily for Cadence to join her.

A moment later, they do, folding themself into the opposite seat.

"So," they say. They are looking Aaliyah in the eye now, for the first time. Their own eyes are dark, sweet, like those of a deer. Aaliyah searches them for any sign of the girl she loved but sees only her own lost face reflected back.

"How long have you had that mod?" she asks at last.

Cadence breaks their gaze, looking down and to the side. They are drumming their long fingers against the table, the music still working its way out of their system—or perhaps they are just anxious. Their hands are wind-chapped, gray with ash. They look like they hurt.

"Eight weeks," Cadence answers. "But most of that's been recovery. These past couple of weekends, singing in the park, have been my first time, you know . . . really trying it out." They touch their throat gently. "I maybe overdid it today."

Aaliyah does not care about this. She is too busy doing the math in her head. The car crash was in April. She moved to Missouri in June. And at some point in . . . October? Reina came back, here, to the exact same place where Aaliyah now finds herself.

Aaliyah is not as religious as her grandmother, but in moments like this, she begins to understand.

"And what made you pick . . . that voice?" Aaliyah asks haltingly.

Cadence meets her eye again. "That's a personal question."

Aaliyah is frustrated. Maybe it was inappropriate of her to ask—she guesses she can see that—but there were never any secrets between her and Reina. She is not used to being denied by this voice.

Although, Aaliyah realizes then, Reina never told her she'd donated her voice. So there was at least one secret.

Aaliyah is beginning to feel sick.

Cadence relents a little, watching her wilt. "I'm non-binary. It was a gender thing for me. I don't care about mods otherwise."

"Oh." Now Aaliyah feels bad for dragging them out of the closet.

"Is that a problem?" Cadence presses.

"No. Of course not. I'm queer as hell. So was she."

"Reina."

"Yes."

Silence stretches between them. It is as if Reina has joined them at the little table and they are both waiting for her to speak.

"Aaliyah!" the barista calls out. Aaliyah is saved. She jumps up from the table to retrieve her drink. They call Cadence's name, too, while she's up there, and she grabs their drink as well. It's a hot chocolate. There is something endearing about that, Aaliyah thinks. It is not Reina's order—Reina liked a caramel latte—but, Aaliyah has to keep reminding herself, Cadence is not Reina.

"Thanks," Cadence murmurs when Aaliyah returns, cupping the drink in their blistered hands. Aaliyah nods wordlessly and sits back down across from them, but suddenly the thought of drinking this coffee, at once too bitter and too sweet, makes her stomach turn.

"So." Cadence takes a sip from their hot chocolate, licks the froth off their upper lip. "Your name's Aaliyah?"

"Yeah, I—yeah," Aaliyah manages. She feels tears threatening again. *God.*

Cadence hesitates. "And you and Reina were . . ."

"Friends." And almost, *almost* something else. Aaliyah abruptly takes a long swallow of her coffee, letting it scald her throat.

"I've never had many friends," Cadence admits. "My brother, I guess. He looks out for me sometimes. I don't know what I'd do if something happened to him." Cadence hesitates again, considering their drink, prodding the bloated marshmallows with a spoon. Then: "Can I ask how—"

"It was a car accident," Aaliyah explains, and then words start pouring out, as burning and painful as the coffee had been pouring in. But it's better this way, better to get it over with. "Eight months ago. We went to this concert together— she loved music, she loved singing—and after she dropped me off at my house, it started raining. Hard. There was this . . . flash flood. Reina never made it home. I couldn't believe it. I still can't. I keep waiting for her to come back. And now"— Aaliyah looks at Cadence—"here you are."

"Wow, that's . . . wow," Cadence murmurs. They swallow, their throat bobbing. They seem to be struggling with whatever words are caught there. "Aaliyah, I am so sorry, but . . . I . . . I'm not her. You know that, right?"

Aaliyah nods, unable to speak. The tears are spilling now, and she lets them. Cadence reaches across to take her hand between theirs, their fingers rough with calluses but their touch gentle.

"I . . . I don't think I should even know too much about her," Cadence continues. "These past few weeks, this mod . . . this is the first time in my life I've ever actually started to feel like *myself*. You know? And I don't want to lose that. I don't want to think of this voice as someone else's."

But it is, Aaliyah screams inside her skull.

But it isn't. This tentative touch is not Reina's, these soft, soulful eyes are not Reina's, and this voice is not Reina's, either, not anymore. It only sounds like her.

Cadence must see the grief breaking across Aaliyah's face, because they withdraw their hands and dig the heels of their palms into their eye sockets in exhaustion.

"Fuck," they mutter. "I'm sorry. This was a bad idea."

"No," Aaliyah says quickly, desperately. "Please, don't go. *I'm* sorry. I'm not—I'm having a hard time today. But it's not your fault. Reina would've loved knowing a part of her helped you. I . . . I want to see you again."

"You want to see *me*, or you want to hear *her*?" Cadence asks shrewdly.

Both—why can't it be both?

"I don't know anyone here," Aaliyah says instead, avoiding the question. "My parents shipped me out to this hellhole to get away from it all, but now I'm just . . . surrounded by strangers. I'm the only Black kid in most of my classes. I'm the wrong kind of queer. You're the first person I've met who I could actually see myself—" Aaliyah does not know why she is saying all this, why she is admitting all this. It is because of Reina's voice, yes, but it is also because of Cadence, their gentleness, their patience. Her throat seizes. "I need a *friend*, Cadence. I don't have a *friend* anymore."

Cadence does not flinch away from her vulnerability. They lean into it, offering up their napkins to wipe away her tears.

"I could use a friend, too," they say softly. "But are you sure that wouldn't just . . . make things harder? For both of us?"

"We can take it a day at a time," Aaliyah says. That is all she can handle anyway. She is not ready to look any further than that, does not want to plan for a future that could be stolen away at any moment.

Cadence seems reassured by this. They even smile for the first time that afternoon, the white of their teeth showing, bright as the snow.

"One day at a time," they agree.

"It used to be nobody could get you to talk. Now you don't shut up," Cadence's brother complains. Cadence has just come out of the shower, wrapped up in a threadbare gray towel, emerging from the steam like a rock star bursting onstage through a cloud of fog. They have been singing at the top of their lungs for the better part of half an hour.

"You're just jealous I sound like Beyoncé now," Cadence says.

Their brother does not know how to respond to this. He is the speechless one these days. "That mod has gone to your head," he mumbles finally, and he pushes his way into the bathroom.

Cadence's brother is right: this mod *has* gone to their head. It has been six months—it is April—and their new voice, which was stiff and sore for weeks, is finally broken in. They can use it freely, without fear of injuring themself, or feeling self-conscious, or making their mother cry. They sing all the time. At first, it was just to test the limits of their mod, but now it is for the joy of it.

Cadence does wonder, sometimes, if that joy is their own or if it's only part of their new programming. They wonder this about a lot of things. They laugh more now. They speak up. They are confident. Maybe this is all the work of some phantom in the machine—but then, maybe, this is just how everyone feels when they are finally themselves.

Cadence is not sure anymore that it matters. Aaliyah has started saying that no one is only themself, that everyone is actually a collage: of the people who raised them, of the people they call their friends, of the poets they read and the singers they listen to. No one is ever really gone, Aaliyah insists. They live on in the component pieces. Cadence is grateful for the color Reina has added to their canvas. She has brought the whole picture into focus. They are not less themself for her gift, but more.

Cadence finishes getting ready for Sunday dinner, jumping into their slim jeans, climbing into their best black hoodie, sliding their feet into their checkered Vans. Aaliyah is coming over, as she has every Sunday night since Christmas.

Even though it has become routine, Cadence still feels a thrill every time.

And this, too, is their own.

"You going to get in here and help me set the table?" Cadence's mother scolds as they jump down the stairs two at a time.

"In a minute!" Cadence promises, because right then, the doorbell rings, Aaliyah is here, and Cadence has always been the one to let her in.

"Admit it. You had fun."

Aaliyah will admit no such thing. Her ears are still ringing from the concert, her throat still sore from roaring with the crowd, but it was a country music concert, and she has a reputation to maintain.

"It was an experience," Aaliyah says.

"'An experience,' okay. I heard you singing along," Reina says slyly, crossing her arms and leaning back against the hood of the car. The night is black around them, and they are huddled on a little island of yellow-brown light filtering down from the streetlight at the end of Aaliyah's driveway. Aaliyah is already later than she said she'd be, and she knows her parents are inside worrying, but she still doesn't want the night to end, not yet.

"Well, I couldn't just leave you hanging," she says.

"You love me that much?"

It is a joke—Reina is smirking—but Aaliyah feels it in her chest: she does love her that much, loves her more than she ever intended to, loves her more than she thinks she can bear. There is a question on her lips, one she has bitten back for she doesn't know how many years. But something about the way Reina looks tonight, the halo of light around her, the shine of her brown skin, has loosened Aaliyah's tongue.

"Reina," she says. "What if I told you that I do love you? Would that . . . would that be okay?"

Reina smiles beautifully at her. She steps forward, closing the distance between them, pulling Aaliyah to her.

The sky breaks open. Rain falls in a spray of bullets, hard and fast. It is one of those sudden spring storms, the kind that come out of nowhere. Reina laughs, water pouring down her face, and presses her forehead to Aaliyah's.

"Ask me again tomorrow," she says, and she lets Aaliyah go.

ON THE TIP OF MY TONGUE

WILLIAM ALEXANDER

I was out for a walk, inspecting tethers and tinkering with small repairs, when Bex called to tell me about you.

"Busy?" Bex asked.

"Yes," I said.

"How busy?"

"A whole entire neighborhood is about to break loose and float away."

"Oh," Bex said. "Which one?"

"Cortado."

"I don't know anyone who lives there. Maybe just let it go?"

"Can't," I said. "They brew the best coffee in Cortado. Tía Cassie would eat my eyeballs if she found out that I could've saved the place and didn't bother."

"Your tía also told you to stop secretly fixing things," Bex pointed out. "Are you out walking alone right now?"

"Shush." I coaxed carbon filaments into braiding themselves back together. "Trying to concentrate here."

"Fine," Bex said. "Hurry, though. I need your help."

I didn't hurry. Filament braids can be fickle. "What's the problem?"

"My cousin gets here soon, from Earth, and then leaves again for a fancy lunar internship. I need you to play host during the layover."

"Why can't you welcome your own cousin to town?" I asked.

"Because," Bex said, "I'm stuck in quarantine."

"What?" I stopped braiding to pay actual attention.

"Took a shift at the docks after school. One of the crates broke. It was supposed to be full of frozen ocean from Europa, except it wasn't really frozen, and it splashed all over me. Now I get to stay in my own little isolation cabin until the doctors are sure I haven't contracted some kind of exciting Europan fish flu."

"Okay," I said. "That's genuinely scary."

"I'm aware," said Bex. "If I mutate into a shark monster, I will probably hunt you down. First I need you to look after my cousin, though."

"Sure," I said. "Text me the details."

"Thanks. I owe you. I'll try not to eat you if I turn into a shark."

Bex's projected face disappeared from inside my helmet visor. Your contact info and shuttle number popped up instead. I didn't have much time before your arrival—just enough to hurry home, climb out of my suit, and meet you at the gates.

I wrapped a temporary patch around Cortado's frayed moorings before I clomped across my hometown's outer hull.

Picture a giant octopus floating between Earth and Luna. The octopus is amusing itself by playing with dozens of yo-yos and simultaneously juggling batons.

This is where I live. Every yo-yo on its tether is a separate spinning neighborhood—or a lone building, or an abandoned ship that docked here more than a hundred years ago and never left. Every baton is a mobile bridge connecting separate places to make them all one place, one city.

Welcome to Eleum.

My family has our own airlock adjacent to Tía Cassie's workshop, because inspecting tethers is her actual job. I'm just an unpaid apprentice / intern / familial source of free labor.

Tía was in the workshop, working late as always, so I told her about the Band-Aid I'd just wrapped around Cortado's tether. She looked up and glared to remind me that I shouldn't ever spacewalk by myself. The festive, sparkly purple pair of eyes she'd picked out for the day made that glare even more unsettling.

Tía's original eyes had been damaged by accidental exposure to vacuum—and by "damaged," I mean they exploded. She'd made new ones out of glass and tiny cameras, which sent signals to a fine mesh she wore over her tongue. Tongues are sensitive. They're good at making sense of complicated signals. The visual bits of her brain had remapped themselves to interpret patterns of electricity crackling across that tongue mesh.

In other words, my auntie taught herself how to taste light.

I loved that about her.

The two of us agreed to properly fix the frayed tether, and soon. Both of us knew that the list of things to fix was very long, though. Innumerable pieces of the city were held together via "temporary" measures. I tried not to think about it too much. Survival always insists that we trust a whole bunch of inherently untrustworthy things.

I made it to the arrival gates in time because I knew all the shortcuts, which meant that I had to run, jump, and glide through varying levels of gravity in rapid succession. That was nausea-inducing, especially when I rushed across Jemisin Bridge, where everyone is supposed to buckle up and tether themselves to the walls between stops. Luckily, I'd forgotten to eat for most of the day, so I didn't have any lunch to lose. That lack of lunch did make me feel light-headed and a little dizzy, though.

Bex didn't warn me that you're gorgeous, which I also found disorienting.

"Hi."

"Hi."

"Welcome to Eleum."

"Thanks."

"Hungry?"

"Starved."

"Okay, I know where we should go first. How long is your layover?"

"Seven hours." You tried not to yawn and sort of squeak-yawned instead. It was unspeakably adorable. "What time is it here?"

"Depends on the neighborhood," I said. "Do you need a place to crash after we eat?"

"No," you insisted. "I need to stay awake. If I don't acclimate to the time they keep at L2, then the lag will be horrible, and right now it's morning over there. Bex promised to keep me caffeinated."

"Then you're lucky I'm here instead. Bex drinks diet soda all day long."

You made an appropriately skeptical face. "Coffee?"

I nodded. "Follow me."

We took the long way to Cortado so we could sample the best bridge food and avoid the more drastic gravity shifts between neighborhoods. Quality street vendors always set up shop on low-speed bridges, with the single exception of the Neci Bridge. Don't ever eat on the Neci. Don't even *cross* the Neci if you can possibly avoid it. Just wait at the bridge stop for the next one to come around.

You paused to stare through every window on our way.

"This place is bonkers."

"True."

"How does it even hold together?"

"Don't ask, or it might fly apart."

"Isn't it already flying apart? Those bridges look like trapeze artists. They grab hold of one station—"

"Neighborhood," I said.

"Neighborhood, then let go to spin around and catch another. Weird to think that we're on a bridge right now while that's happening." You took a bite of spicy elote and got bits of squishy corn stuck in your teeth. "Where did the name Eleum come from? Is it Spanish?"

"Portuguese," I said. "Sort of. It isn't a word—just a letter and a number stuck together. Ele-um. L1. Lagrange Point One."

"Aha," you said. "The first of five magic spots where the gravity wells of the moon and the planet call a truce and cancel each other out. Almost."

"Exactly." I couldn't decide whether or not to tell you about the corn in your teeth. "Wait. What do you mean by 'almost'?"

"L1 points aren't very stable," you said, explaining my own home to me. "They wobble more than L4s or L5s. Those would have been better spots to build a great big space city."

I got a little defensive, even though I'd just joked about this whole place flying apart—and even though I was one of the few people who knew how many Band-Aids kept that from happening. "Nobody planned to build this great big space city. Eleum just grew. A little refueling station turned into a fuel refinery for all the lunar ice, and then a shipyard, and then it needed a town to house everyone who worked long shifts at the yards and the docks. New craft took off. Old craft came to rest and stayed. Everything kludged together, like rocks and dust collecting to grow a whole new planet—or like old planetside cities that sprang up wherever river met ocean. All of that happened *here*. It couldn't have happened anywhere else. I don't care how stable L5 thinks it is."

"Okay, grumpyface." You took another bite, which made the tooth situation worse. "I like it when you defend the honor of your city."

"Good." I plucked two toothpicks from a nearby stall counter, gave one to you, and picked my own teeth as a hint. You got it. I tried not to look, but it was oddly mesmerizing to watch you coax offending corn kernels out from where they'd gotten stuck.

"So," I said, "you're headed to L2 from here?"

You grinned a luminous grin. "Floating on the far side of Luna. That's where they keep the really big radio telescopes, shielded from all of this traffic and noise. Earth and Luna like to talk to each other. And look at each other. The big lunar cities are all on this side, gazing downwell. I get to look upward and outward at everything else instead! Or at least I'll get to fetch the coffee for all the real astrophysicists who live there. Still, I can't wait." You set your toothpick inside a bin so it wouldn't float away and get inhaled accidentally during the next bridge-wide gravity dip. "Speaking of coffee, I was promised some. There's a stall right over there."

"Undrinkable," I said. "We'll need to switch bridges at the next stop to get to Cortado."

The absolute best of the Cortado cafés is on the downtown side of the neighborhood, in what used to be the cargo hold of a derelict shuttle, so that's where we went to sip the first of several cafecitos.

I confessed that the neighborhood was staying put because of a bandage that I'd only just wrapped around its mooring. You seemed delighted by the danger rather than alarmed. Then you quoted the first line of my favorite Zorro movie. I had no choice but to say the next line. We kept going, swapping characters back and forth and reciting the entire thing across our café table. Neither of us cheated by calling up the script to scroll inside our eyes. I could tell by the way you looked at me the whole time and never hesitated over a line, not even when Cortado shifted to accommodate the passage of another neighborhood.

I knew the shift was coming, though I'm not sure how I knew. Cortado isn't where I live and sleep. I didn't have sea legs for these particular streets and corridors. Eleum doesn't move like predictable clockwork, either—this place moves like a blissfully confident octopus onstage. Sometimes the background hum of kinetic motion does make sense to me, though, and this was one of those times. I knew what my city was going to do next, which made me want to stick out my tongue at your comment that L1 points were never truly stable. I also wanted to warn you, but I didn't, because right at that moment you were halfway through Friar Felipe's monologue and I really didn't want to interrupt. Instead of saying something, I took your hand and squeezed before the lights dimmed and the gravity got weird.

You squeezed back, finished the friar's speech despite the

shifting gravity, and didn't let go of my hand for the rest of the night. I had to use my left hand to pick up my drink and almost spilled intensely sugary espresso all over myself.

After seven hours of walking and talking and laughing and caffeinating, I got you to the departure gates on time—barely, because I insisted that we go wide around the Neci Bridge to find a better breakfast.

"Bye."

"Bye."

"Thanks for staying up all night," you said.

"Have fun watching the rest of the universe."

"I'll need to keep radio silent at L2," you said. "That's the whole point of L2. So you won't hear from me for a couple of months, but I'll be coming back this way after that. Here's the shuttle number." Your words stuck together, like you weren't sure what order they were supposed to go in. Were you nervous? During the past seven hours, you hadn't seemed nervous about anything—not even exploring an accidental and probably inadvisable city held together by duct tape and hope—but now you sounded nervous about me. "See you then?"

I squeezed your hand. "See you then. Unless Eleum flies apart first."

"Try to keep that from happening."

"I'll do my best."

I'm not sure when the talking stopped and the kissing started. Then the kissing stopped, and you flew away to the far side of the moon.

Tía Cassie fixed me with a look when I stumbled back into her workshop. Her latest pair of eyes glinted gold around narrow pupils, like a cat's. I bet she used real gold leaf to make those shiny irises.

"Whose orbit are you in, kid?" Tía asked.

I ignored the question because I didn't like the image. I'd never been pulled into anyone else's orbit before. I used to be safe, secure, and stable in my own personal L-point, beholden to no other gravity, but then you warped space-time all around me. That was fantastic while you were still here, and much less fantastic the instant you left. Now it felt like I was falling. Objects in orbit are always falling.

"Need work," I said.

"Need sleep," Tía insisted. "No wandering around outside until after you get some rest."

I grumbled and agreed to stay out of my suit, and out of the airlock, but I didn't leave the workshop. I knew I couldn't sleep. Too wired. My whole body seemed to be vibrating at the frequency of a completely separate universe.

I picked up one of Tía's extra eyeballs. The iris was bright red and spiky. "Some people think you spliced your DNA with alien strains from Europa and that's why you've got otherworldly eyes."

"Started that rumor myself," she told me. "Helps filter out the folks who aren't worth talking to."

Mentioning alien strains from Europa reminded me that

I should check on Bex in quarantine. I didn't, though. Bex would ask about you, and I wasn't sure what to say.

Remember that moment when Cortado shifted and I took your hand with all the confidence of a juggling octopus acrobat? I missed that feeling. I missed knowing what the kinetic motion all around us really meant. Now I couldn't parse any of it, even here at home in Tía's workshop, surrounded by my own neighborhood.

I set the demonic red eye back in its case. "Hey, Tía?"

"Hm?"

"About that tongue mesh that your eyes talk to . . ."

"What about it?"

"Do you think it could process other kinds of signals?"

She fixed me with a look. "What kinds, exactly?"

"I don't know," I said, even though I did know. "Information that our senses don't usually have access to. Weather patterns on Jupiter, maybe."

Tía put down her tools and closed her eyes. (It takes extra concentration to speak when you're also using your tongue to see.) "Why would you want a permanent hurricane simulation messing with your taste buds?"

"Bad example." I took a breath before asking what I really wanted to ask. "How about motion sensor data from all over Eleum? Tensor strength in different neighborhood tethers. A live schedule of every bridge."

"Why?"

Here's what I didn't say: *Because it turns out that L1 points aren't as stable as I always thought, which means Eleum is even more precarious and wobbly than we already knew, and right now I feel just as wobbly. I want my equilibrium back.*

Here's what I actually said: "Because it might help make our repair work more efficient. Do you think it's possible to learn how to taste that sort of thing?"

"Sounds like a headache," Tía said. "But sure, theoretically. Tongues are erogenous zones. Already wired for extra attention and complex input."

Thinking about tongues as erogenous zones would not help me recover my lost equilibrium. "Can you show me how to wire up a sensor mesh?"

Tía waved me away and went back to work. "Later. Get some rest. You've got school tomorrow. Come find me after that if you still want to taste the way our city moves."

The mesh on my tongue tasted faintly metallic. Networked signals from all around Eleum tickled like the fizzy bubbles in Bex's terrible soda. I kept practicing anyway. Complex sensations danced inside my mouth. None of it meant anything—not until late one night when I went out walking alone.

It was dark. Luna loomed to one side, lunar cities glowing against the dusky blanket of the new moon. Eleum danced in the in-between. I watched my city move all around me, loving the sheer, ridiculous bravado that it took for us to even exist out here.

Then my perspective shifted. Kinesthesia expanded. My entire sense of self became city-size.

I don't know how long I stood there, savoring how it felt

to move like a massive space cephalopod yo-yo champion of a metropolis. Eventually, my morning alarm went off, which broke the hypnotic flow. Signals from Eleum turned back into background fizzing in my mouth. I clicked my tongue, switched the mesh off, and went inside to find some coffee.

"My cousin's coming back soon," Bex said, newly released from quarantine with no icky symptoms of ichthyic transformation.

"Mm-hmm," I answered, trying to act like I hadn't been counting the days.

"I'm kinda busy, though," Bex said. "Think you can play host again without me?"

YES, I thought.

"Sure," I said.

Three bridges shut down the night before your shuttle arrived, so Tía Cassie and every other techie I knew got diverted to round-the-clock bridge repair—everyone except me, because I was still too young to work an official shift.

Tía offered to sneak me in anyway. I politely declined. That surprised her. "Kid, you were building model bridges before you could walk. Now you don't want to tinker with the real thing?"

I mumbled something about having stuff to do.

With the bridges down, I couldn't reach your arrival gate in time, so we arranged by text to meet in Cortado. You got lost, because downloadable maps don't ever hold still in Eleum. I also got lost, because the broken bridges made everything wonky. We tried and failed to joke about it, texting our unfunny frustrations at each other as everything conspired to keep us apart. These were the first words we'd shared since you'd flown into L2's bubble of silent contemplation.

I turned on the tongue mesh and closed my eyes. I needed to sense how the neighborhoods were navigating around one another. That should have been easy, like touching a fingertip to my nose with my eyes closed. It wasn't easy, though. Getting both of us back into that little shuttle café in Cortado took almost two hours.

We didn't kiss hello. The moment when we should have passed so quickly that I didn't even notice until it was already gone. You grabbed us a table. I fetched us the coffee. Then I realized I still had a mesh of tiny sensors stuck all over the surface of my tongue, which would probably make kissing awkward. Thinking about it made me click my enmeshed tongue against the roof of my mouth, which switched the sensors on. I'm not sure why I did that. Maybe it was habit. Maybe I wanted to feel confidently city-size while sitting across from you.

That was when you leaned across the table to kiss me.

I'm really sorry about what happened next.

My city-sense tingled. I felt motion in every direction, and then I recognized the Cortado tether. I felt it weaken. My Band-Aid was breaking. Momentum would send this whole neighborhood hurtling into the sky when that tether broke, and the worst part was that we wouldn't sail clear. The shipyards at the outer edge of town would block our way. I could feel it. Careening into that would be like hitting the city with a comet from the inside, and then all of Eleum would fly apart. I felt like my whole body was about to fly apart.

That's why I panicked when you kissed me.

That's why I bit down hard on the tip of your tongue.

I'm really, really sorry. I wish I'd said so at the time. I should have paused to check in, make sure you were okay, and offer you a napkin to dab your bleeding tongue wound. Instead, I stood on our table and shouted, "Everybody out!"

No one moved. You'd think that people who'd lived their whole lives in an accidental space city would be less reluctant to recognize emergencies, but nope. *There's a hull breach? That sucks. Let me finish my coffee before I start caring.*

Eduardo, the owner, shouted back at me from behind the counter. "What's the problem?"

I didn't know how to explain. *Fear me, for I have become one with Eleum! I taste the city electric, and also its doom . . . and also the blood of my companion here, because our second date is going very badly so far. Heed my prophecy and flee this place!*

Instead of explaining, I pointed at two antique suits on the wall. "Do those still work?"

"No idea," Eduardo said. "They're just for decoration. Came with the place when my grandparents bought it. Now get down from my table, please."

I got down from the table. "You have to go. Hurry. Trust me—I'm on the repair crew, and you have to get out of here."

Eduardo seemed unfazed and unimpressed. "If you were really on the crew, you'd be fixing bridges right now."

"Eddie, I promise you this café will decompress in minutes. Please go before that happens. Find a shelter far from the outer hull."

"Don't ever call me Eddie," Eduardo said. He still left. So did everyone else—everyone except for you.

I tried and failed to get you to follow them. "Go. I can fix this, but I need to go outside first."

"There are two of those suits," you pointed out.

Watching you climb inside a bulky suit shouldn't have made my mouth go dry, but it did. Why would putting clothes on remind me of taking them off? The distraction and the sudden lack of spit switched off my city-sense. My body felt me-size again. I awkwardly stuffed myself into the other suit.

"So what's going on?" you asked while trying to figure out how the helmet clasps worked.

"Remember the Band-Aid I told you about before?"

"The one that keeps this part of the station in place?"

"City, not station. And yes. That one. It's breaking."

"How do you know?"

"Tell you later." I still felt too tongue-tied to explain properly.

"What happens when it breaks?"

"We ram into the shipyards."

"That sounds bad."

"Very."

"So what should we do about it?"

"We'll cut ourselves loose."

You seemed understandably skeptical of my brilliant

plan. I noticed a little bit of blood smeared across your bottom lip, and I wanted to wipe it away, but I also didn't want to remind you why it was there.

"Isn't breaking loose what we're trying to avoid?" you reasonably asked.

"Can't be avoided," I said, "but if we cast off right now, before the shipyards get in our way, we'll sail clear instead of crashing."

"Okay, then. Let's go." You figured out how to seal your helmet. Then you reached over and sealed mine.

I mumbled a quick litany for ancestral blessings, hoped that our eyeballs weren't about to explode, and wondered how you could possibly trust me enough to spontaneously spacewalk together in derelict suits. Then I rewired the old cargo bay doors to open for the first time in generations. Several cups of half-drunk coffee got sucked into open space, but thankfully our eyeballs stayed put.

The two of us climbed outside. We clomped across Cortado's outer hull. I wanted to compliment the way you handled yourself in a suit, but the old radios didn't work. I wrote a text instead, fingers tapping an imaginary keyboard, fingernail phone implants figuring out what I wanted to say. Then I second-guessed the unsent compliment and erased it. Then I wished I'd sent it anyway, because it was true. You really do know how to move in a suit.

We found the tether. Its emergency release was broken, because of course it was, so we pried open the access panel.

I couldn't see the shipyards from our downtown-facing

vantage point, so I switched my city-sense back on. I needed to check whether or not we were still within the window for a clean breakaway. Maybe we were already too late.

At first, the fizzing signals made no sense. Then the fizz meant far too much. Disrupted bridge patterns cluttered up my head. Eleum and I were equally off-kilter. That was the whole problem. I knew how it felt to be a space octopus on the verge of dropping the lit torches and chain saws it was juggling.

Our window hadn't closed yet, though. I pulled a live wire loose and zapped the tether with it, because pulses of electricity can remind carbon filaments how to unbraid themselves.

The single tether became many separate strands. The mooring broke free of its weakened Band-Aid on the far side.

Cortado sailed clear.

We waved at the yardies, close enough to see horrified faces behind their helmet visors as we barely missed the ship-yards, and then Eleum seemed to fall away from us rather than the other way around.

The city looked small from a distance. I'd never thought of home as small before. I'd also never left before.

The very last echoes of my tongue signals fizzled down to nothing.

Then you bumped into me. I thought it was an accident until you did it again. I could see your face, eyes wide and delighted, and suddenly the outer hull of runaway Cortado felt like solid ground.

MELANITIS

JUNAUDA
PETRUS-NASAH

WHEN I heard the news on the radio that the seventh FAN was murdered by police, I was staring into the bathroom mirror envisioning myself with a rose-petal-pink dandelion Afro. My phone buzzed against my thigh and there were two texts. One from Ryder and one from Desi. Ryder wanted to know if he could come through and talk. Desi's message was a picture of two different tubes of pink hair dye in her brown manicured hand. I left Ryder's text on read and responded to Desi's with three cotton candy and two unicorn emojis.

I brought up the idea of cutting my hair a couple of weeks ago, after I told my folks I also didn't feel my gender fit me. The thing is, I've had dreadlocs since I was a baby and my parents have them, too. Our locs signify our little tribe—all of our manes are each other's pride in a trifecta kind of way. My hair thick and twisted into long, twirling cords by my father's fingers. My locs was how I was known. "Amari with the dreads." My dreads, able to wrap around me like a blanket, made me look like I was equally the child of my mother and father.

A feeling in a dream changed something for me, though. I had a dream last week that my hair was cut close and soft to my scalp. I was in a yard that felt like my grandma's in Milwaukee, one of my favorite places in the world, but looked completely different. In the dream, I was looking at the sky and it looked like watery mirrors, and when I saw my reflection, I was my own self and no one else.

"So how did it feel like in the dream? Were you sad your hair was gone?" Desi asked me when we were talking on the phone the night after the dream. I was lying in my bed, under my covers, and imagining her on the other side of the line twirling her sea-colored braids between her fingers. I felt myself hold my breath, listening to her voice. We had begun calling each other instead of just texting about two months ago.

"Not really. But when I woke up, I felt my head and it was weird to feel my dreads still there, you know? I expected to feel the little chickadee fuzz head I had."

"That would look fire, Amari. What color was it though? You know how dream colors look different from real-life colors?"

"Hmmm, how do I describe it?" I really thought about it. "You know the color of strawberry ice cream? But with strawberries you picked, churned by your favorite auntie." I lay with my locs on my chest, watching them float with my inhalations.

"Can I help with your hair color? I wanna try and make it look strawberry for you. You gon' look sexy." My tummy dipped when she said that all casual, that I would look sexy. I closed my eyes and imagined my head in her lap and her hands in my hair.

"Amari, I got to go, honey," my mom said, suddenly outside the bathroom door and pulling me out of my thoughts about Desi's hands.

"Come in, Ma."

She whooshed in and landed on the toilet with the exhale of relief that comes when you been holding your pee a couple minutes too long. She was still in her work clothes from teaching. When she was done, she washed her hands next to me. She paused and looked at the both of us in the mirror, her locs on top of her head in a bun while mine hung long and lanky down my back.

"I bet you are going to have a cute little head," she said, glancing at my locs with a wistful smile, then squeezed me to her. With a sigh, she started changing out of her work clothes to get into something more comfortable.

"Let me get on to my research. This whole Cha'Darius situation is already getting intense."

"White folks acting like they the first ones ever to be Black and oppressed. Big ol' crybabies," my grandmother said with an irritated sigh, back when the

whole outbreak first happened and the wealthy with their newly browned teenagers marched in the streets, demanding the government protect their rights. Not rights for Black or Brown people, mind you, but for FANS. They didn't want to be profiled or harassed because of the color of their skin, because deep down they were white and still wanted to be treated as such.

The news of the police killing of another FAN caused a national frenzy that would be unavoidable in most houses, but especially mine, with my mom's research and writing on the subject and its impact on Black people. Our living room became a situation room. My mom plopped down next to me with chips and guacamole for us to snack on. I was on the couch, drawing in my sketchbook some anime of myself with my new hair and comparing it to the countless ones I'd drawn of me with my locs.

My mom's eyes were glued to the television as she set up her laptop, notebook, and pens to ready herself for all the notes she would be taking as the events unfolded that evening and in the weeks to come. My mom considers hours-long CNN binges on anything FAN-related as "academic research." One of her research focuses is comparing how the media portrays the victims of a police homicide differently if they were a FAN or BBB.

On the television screen flashed a picture of a smiling dark brown man with gray eyes and a close-shaved head, his arm around a pretty brown-skinned Black woman. They were holding a light-skinned child carrying a stuffed pink flamingo.

Underneath, the screen said, "Police shoot unarmed man in front of his parents' suburban home." You had to look real close at the man to see that he was a FAN and not BBB. Some FANs were like that. I looked at the little boy in his arms, who looked like a perfect mixture of both of his parents, his tan skin being the only tell that one of his parents was not BBB.

FAN was slang that real Black folks, aka Black by Birth (BBB) folks, used to describe the group of people who got dark from Melanitis—a side effect of parental Moremipin use. FAN stood for "Fake Ass Negros," which was also a way that we distinguished them from us, the BBBs or, as we young Black folks call ourselves, RANs (Real Ass Negros). White folks afflicted with Melanitis found the term FAN insensitive and derogatory. Black people found the term appropriate (and funny), especially given how white people were starting to experience the anxiety of how it feels to walk in the world with Black skin. One byproduct of the Melanitis plague was an increase in white fragility.

I looked at my phone and saw that Ryder already texted me three times since I checked an hour ago. I still didn't want to deal with it. Some Black folks got that one white friend who got Melanitis and Ryder is mine. He always got anxious when a FAN was killed and wanted to talk about it. He would apologize for taking my time and say he didn't wanna be a "typical white kid with Melanitis," but then he would go on and on about his fears, about feeling paranoid and anxious because folks were treating him "negatively" for "no reason." I would listen and then be feeling like . . . so what? I had experienced things like that since I was five years old.

Dealing with his fragile FAN feelings was becoming harder for me, to be honest. Watching him sulk and complain about his experience of "looking different," as he calls his new brown-skindedness. How do you talk to someone who is sad and confused because they look more like you and misses being a regular degular ass white boy? The more melanated he gets, the less I feel like we get each other, which is ironic, I guess. And Ryder is from a "woke" liberal family, which is more annoying somehow.

Either way, I have a lot of figuring out right now with my own self. I ain't even told Ryder about me feeling Desi. I started sketching an anime of Desi with her braids extending into a deep-sea scene full of coral. I've been wondering what Desi thinks of me. The anticipation of having her over and hooking my hair up is making me smile, and I can't even help it. Over the last couple of weeks, we've become closer than I am with anyone else in our crew.

One day Desi called me out of the blue to ask what I use to twist my locs and if I keep a dream journal. It took me off guard, since people usually text and don't really call me all like that . . . but when she called, it made me wanna tell her everything about me. And to be honest, I always thought Desi was dope. So after that call, that's when I got to really know her and let her know me. After a while we was talking all the time.

My mama going off on the television brought me back to reality. "Of course this was gonna happen. This FAN was still walking around with the assumption of being trusted and protected like it was when he was a little white boy." She dipped her chip in our pre-dinner guac and wrote some more notes.

The face of the victim, Chad "Cha'Darius" Anderson, was flashing on the screen again, both before Melanitis and after: as a white teen and then next as a grown "black" man. "Mmmmhmm. Same person, same soul, but one skin will protect him, while the other will get him killed," my mom said. She realized that thought sounded deep and went quiet while she wrote it down.

The reporter began interviewing the same brown-skinned woman from the photo. She was stunned and blinking like she was still trying to focus on something in front of her face that she couldn't quite make out. Under her face, it said, "Danitria Henry, fiancée of Chad 'Cha'Darius' Anderson."

"I told Cha'Darius to stay inside today . . . Stop trying to get his parents to understand him and come to our wedding. He was so nervous, he was probably just trying to get the nerve and kept circling the block." Her voice choked at the thought and she began to sob.

Danitria's mother, Pam, stepped in. "I had a feeling, but he didn't listen. I have told him, you can't think like a white boy with the police, not how you look now . . ." Pam was talking as though he was still alive to hear her warning.

"Over and over again, I would tell him like I would tell my sons, when cops stop you, this is how you have to act. Do exactly as they say, no sudden movements, give them your license slowly . . ." Her mama said these instructions like she was explaining how to feed a rabid wolf without it gobbling your hand, knowing that it probably would anyway. Danitria stood by her mother, clearly still in shock. She had the kinda fake lashes that were dramatic, like a baby doll's, thick and dark, but her eyes were far away and heavy.

"Cha'Darius was shot by an armed police officer who had been called by his family's neighbors," said the head reporter on the scene. "The officer shot him within twenty-five seconds of his arrival on the scene."

My mom sighed and took a break from her notes to begin making dinner. She went to the kitchen and bent down to look inside the fridge. She filled my arms up with garlic, kale, sweet potato, and onions and motioned me off to start cutting. She leaned on the counter, eyes glued to the screen with full attention. My phone buzzed and it was from Ryder, again. It said, "Hey Amari, you gonna be home later?" I put my phone back in my pocket and went back to helping make dinner.

My mom teaches at the University of Minnesota and researches the safety, visibility, and civil rights of Black by

Birth people since the Melanitis outbreak. Her main focus is on how Black people are experiencing and asserting sovereignty in their own Blackness. Especially because suddenly all of these privileged white people are beginning to become melanated in unpredictable ways and gentrifying Blackness.

"Look at this kid Chad, ahem . . . 'Cha'Darius,' from the rich suburbs," my mom said as she joined me in prepping the vegetables for a moment. "I bet he and his family were estranged, like most of these FANs who decide to leave the white world behind. The Dolezal effect is what they are calling it, which I find an annoying term, even if it somewhat fits the phenomenon. They probably didn't understand why he would rather live as a 'black' man than attempt any fairness retention procedure." She stopped chopping and went to grab a bottle of wine.

"Being Black is the new black for some of these FANs," I said, and it was. For as many FANs who were mortified by their browned skin, others got Kardashian with it and treated it like the newest accessory or status symbol.

"Being Black is all fun and games until someone gets they ass shot by police," my mom said with a shrug.

Many of them tried everything to stay pale-faced. Pasty and bright concealers and foundations that made them look like they were literal clowns doing white face. A whole line of "fairness retention" cosmetics was invented in the pursuit of keeping one's whiteness. A lot of the products were either really toxic or scams sold on Amazon and used in thirsty desperation. It became common to see white kids from the suburbs rubbing on face-bleaching creams outlawed in Nigeria, India, and Trinidad but procured by a well-connected parent.

Back in front of the TV while our dinner cooked, my mom and I got caught right back up in the drama.

"We are on the scene, and we are talking with Andrew Olson, one of the neighbors on the same block as the Anderson family. Mr. Olson, how do you feel about this police shooting happening in your community?"

"I never imagined anything like this happening here. This, I mean . . . Wow . . . Chad was a great kid. He and my son were on the same Little League team. I still can't believe he's gone . . ." His voice trailed off and his eyes darted around, holding back tears.

"Why do you think the police were called on him, if he grew up on this block?" asked Houa Vang, a reporter with a silver streak in her hair and bright fuchsia lips, while holding the microphone steady in front of Mr. Olson.

"We are good people here. I mean, Chad, he was a good guy, too. I mean, he could have just . . . if he only wore makeup, or kept his hair long and did the laser thing to be lighter, maybe, uh . . . All we saw was a suspicious Black man circling the block . . . suspiciously. We didn't think it was Chad, obviously. He is from our community, but you know he looks different now and . . . wouldn't that make anyone . . . suspicious?"

Ms. Vang broke character as a reporter and rolled her eyes. My mom clapped at the television.

"So if he used White-alicious or whatever that scary, toxic bleaching cream is or wore makeup, y'all wouldn't call the cops?" my mom said, rolling her eyes.

"Remember when them rich people were acting like Moremipin was ethical medical freedom? Lobbying for it and all of that. I wonder what these parents think now that they kids are turning Black! And Blackity, Black BLACK! And being TREATED Black at that."

I couldn't tell if my mom was horrified or gloating or a little of both.

"Speaking of . . . How is Ryder doing?"

I didn't answer right away. I wasn't expecting her to bring him up. Me and Ryder been tight since we was babies. Our moms were both obsessive academics in the gender and women's studies department. We spent nights at each other's house, and when his parents got divorced, he was at our house all of the time and we got real tight. Things changed a little when we went to high school and got different friends, but we always fam. Since he got the 'nitis, though, he really began struggling. A corny white boy struggle but his struggle nonetheless.

"I don't know how Ryder is doing. We ain't really been talking." My mom looked up, and I could tell she was not surprised.

I didn't want to talk about Ryder. "How is Ms. Amber doing?" I asked her as she locked the top on the pressure cooker. Ms. Amber is one of my mama's few white friends, and Ryder's mama. They met while pregnant with us in graduate school and bonded over academics, politics, and being new moms. They were close but things ain't been the same with them, either, since Ryder melanated. My mom took a sip of wine and paused a second before she responded.

"I . . . I haven't. I mean, what can I say? She lied about taking Moremipin. Like how disgusting and elitist is that? You wanna be seen as a down white woman, but then also slide your rich privilege on the low?" I moved to sit down at the kitchen table, knowing I'd touched a nerve and should settle in. "We used to talk shit about these rich white women taking this weird drug, and all this time she was ensuring some kind of edge for her son," she said, and I could see that my mom was really hurt. She grazed her hand along my locs and looked at me.

"Like, how can you say you love me or my child, or any non-rich person, when you are willing to pay top dollar to keep yourselves above us?" she said, looking into my eyes.

It was a supplement taken by expectant mothers, and doses cost $10,000 to $100,000, depending on the strain. Some Moremipin babies were able to read by age one and learn complex math by age three, but these instances were rare and only in cases where fourth and fifth doses were administered. It was *marketed as a high-end birth supplement to the rich and famous (and aspirational middle class) but eventually became known as a performance-enhancing drug, and after a few years it was banned. Most of the parents who took Moremipin argued that they wanted to give their children a leg up. Just like a top-tier preschool or expensive tutors, Moremipin was seen by the rich as a necessary precondition for their children's success.*

Some white folks began melanating, or "browning," due to Melanitis as early as thirteen or as late as twenty-one. Melanitis affects all genders, but cis boys made up 89 percent of cases. Millions and millions have been invested in treatments and cures for the disease since the initial outbreak five years ago. They even established support groups for FANs. Some Melanitis sufferers and their parents felt they were even more oppressed than BBB people and thus should be able to check the "Black" box for college applications. Yup, they tried it.

The TV stayed on until Dad got home, just in time for dinner. At his salon, the news about the death of Cha'Darius was a hot topic of debate among the Black clients and staff. Over dinner he insisted we talk about something other than the FAN murder. I knew the conversation would turn to my hair and the recent talk we'd had about my gender.

"Amari, but I was thinking . . . ain't locs kinda for

everyone? Not a gender thing, really? Me and your mama both have locs." My dad spooned vegan stew into his bowl and sprinkled some chopped cilantro on top.

"Yeah, I know. It's not just about me and my gender. I can't explain it—I'm just ready for this," I said with my locs under my hoodie and down my back.

"You ready to let it go?" he asked. "You've grown them your whole life, though." He said this like I didn't know it to be true.

"Yes, Dad. I'm ready, ready. Like, feel-a-breeze-on-my-whole-head ready," I said, an annoyed look on my face. He looked at me and chuckled and nodded in the way he does when I amuse him. Like I finally said something that broke through his own thick crown of locs.

"I see. You're becoming new for yourself," he said. "Like a rite of passage. We should do a ritual for your locs, then."

"About that. Actually Desi is going to do it. She's going to help me cut it into a fade . . . and dye it a strawberry ice cream color," I said, only wondering how he would feel about it as the words came out of my lips. He looked up at me, and from his eyes, I could tell this was a step further then maybe he expected the whole situation to go. He looked disappointed but then caught his face and tried to look open-minded. My mom looked at both of us and filled up the quiet space.

"Strawberry ice cream color?" She looked at me like she was trying to see it, then nodded once the image settled in her mind. My dad was just quiet, but I still felt him. Hair is like his soul's work. He is a magician with the hair of Black people, all of our textures and kinks. I thought of all of the years that he spent washing, moisturizing, and twisting my hair. I realized even though I was ready for a new vibe, it maybe was a step too far for me, too.

"Actually. I think a ritual would be right. And having you help me cut them off would be dope. You always hook me up." He looked at me with a little bit of relief and smiled.

"Amari, thank you for letting me do it. I'll leave you with a little 'fro, and you and your friend can experiment from there."

After dinner I sat on a stool in the kitchen, and my mom wrapped me in a towel and set a mirror up for me to look at myself. My dad grabbed his scissors and looked at me through the mirror and smiled. I inhaled and then exhaled as he cut a foot of my hair off. I instantly felt like I was floating. I closed my eyes, and with each cut, I felt a little more fluffy and tingly. After it was all cut off, I looked at myself in the mirror. My parents watched me.

"What do you think, honey?" my dad asked, nodding at his work.

"Do you like it, 'Mari?" My mom was looking nervous, waiting for me to say something. I put my hands all around my head and felt my Afro and turned my face around in the mirror. I could see my cheeks and the shape of my head.

"I . . . feel good. Dang. This is everything, Dad . . ." I said and meant it. My mom and dad began picking up my hair. I took a pile of it in my fists and felt the energy humming off of it.

"We are going to take good care of this until you decide what kind of ritual you want to do with it," my dad said.

Later, I stood under the shower and felt my head, and it felt free. There were parts of me that I was learning about that felt like me and only me, not my mom or my dad. Like they wouldn't even understand. And I liked it.

Blick! Bop! Bdrick!

I heard some stones thrown at my window, and I knew it was Desi here to help me for the last step. I headed to my window to let her know I'd be right down. When I looked out, my heart sank. Ryder's brown face was below my window peeking from under his hoodie.

Ryder and I sat outside on my stoop. I didn't know what to say, and to be honest, I was feeling some kinda way that he popped up on me.

"It's good to see you. Sorry I dropped by all extra. I couldn't get a hold of you," he said.

"My bad. I was busy," I said while looking up into the big maple leaves above us. It was awkwardly quiet between Ryder and me. It was never that way before. I watched the rustling leaves. "So, Ryder, what's up?"

"I just wanted to talk. Did you hear about that man who got shot outside his parents' house? Cha'Darius?" he said, looking into my eyes. I gave him a side-eye.

"You already know. My mama been on it," I said. Ryder started wringing his hands and just being quiet in a way I wasn't in the mood for.

"So you came here to be all quiet?" I asked him.

"No. It's not just that, Amari . . . Today something happened to me," he said.

"What happened?"

"I was walking in my dad's new neighborhood in the suburbs that him and Meghan moved to last month, and I was followed by two white guys. At first I assumed they were just walking. But then they turned on the same block as me and then followed me to the cul-de-sac my dad lives on."

"That sounds scary," I said, seeing he was still shook.

"They yelled at me that I don't look like I belong there. I was about to run, but just then, Meghan came out for her evening run and told them I was her stepson and had Melanitis. It was terrifying, Amari. And then I came home and heard about Cha'Darius," he said, still unsettled, while I felt myself start to get hot on the inside.

What did he want me to say? Poor thing. What a terrifying brush with almost oppression? Good thing you ain't really BBB?

"Good thing Meghan could vouch for you, that you weren't a RAN," I said, not able to hold back my irritation.

"I know . . . I mean, it's not cool, but they were probably going to beat me up," he said, sensing my lack of concern but not feeling my hurt. I was tired of him not seeing how oblivious he is to the ways Black folks have dealt with this stuff and worse forever, including me. He never understood my Blackness and I don't get his Melanitis ass.

"I bet you they got real nice to you after they learned

you were a white boy. Imagine if you were a RAN—how that woulda panned out real different," I said.

"I know, but I was freaked out, okay? This is all new to me. And then that dude Cha'Darius is dead and he wasn't even doing anything. He was going to see his parents and the police shot him for no reason." When those words left his lips, I thought of all of the Black people killed for no reason. Sandra Bland. Tamir Rice. Breonna Taylor. Fred Hampton. People that even in his melanation he still didn't feel for.

I looked at my old best friend. The kid who I used to play dinosaurs and make poop jokes with. And the one who now apparently misses his privileged white body, on some level, even though he would never say that. I been Black since I came out my mama's you know what. Not because my parents were rich and thirsty enough to take Moremipin. Even if some of these kids feel like they are horribly oppressed in their new black skin—getting the cops called on them for things they used to get away with or being stared at in public—don't make it the same.

Just then a car pulled up, and I saw the door open and Desi stepped out. She said a "Thanks, girl" behind her back to whoever dropped her off. She walked up and saw Ryder and looked between the two of us. I went and gave her a hug.

"Hey, Desi, this is Ryder." They both greeted each other politely. "You can just slide inside. My room is the last one on the right. My parents know you coming." Desi headed inside and then it was just me and Ryder alone again. We looked at each other and I saw someone familiar but also really different.

"Ryder, I know it's hard seeing people who are like you getting hurt and killed for no reason . . ." I breathed out and let go of something.

"But to be real, I can't hold this for you right now. I gotta take care of me and this is some white stuff right here and y'all gotta figure it out, bro," I said, my hands deep in my hoodie's pockets.

"Sorry, I've clearly annoyed you with my problems," Ryder said, fighting back tears and getting on his bike.

"You're gonna be aight. Look at Black people. We been Black since forever!"

Ryder rode away and I watched him leave.

When I came into my room, Desi was on my bed playing a game on her phone. I told her to close her eyes, that I had a surprise. I unzipped my hoodie and revealed myself all shea buttered up in my pajamas with my Afro glowing with product.

"You can look now." She removed her hands from her eyes and looked at me. I was wondering what she would think when she saw me and my little 'fro. I looked so different to myself. I'd spent a long time in the mirror massaging the conditioner into my wet, soft hair, getting used to the new sensation.

"My dad did it," I said.

"Damn, your dad hooked you up," she said. Her dark brown eyes sparkled, and I felt seen by her, in ways I have never felt seen.

"The shape is perfect. He did a way better job than what

I woulda done. You looked fly with your locs, boo, don't get me wrong. But this cut . . ." She inspected me while circling around my dome, then leaned back and smiled at me.

"It's easier to see your really sweet face, turns out," she said, looking in my eyes, lingering. I like when she does that. She changed from her work outfit into some pajamas she borrowed from me and plopped down next to me on my bed.

"I'm still gonna dye it for you, though. I can't stop thinking of your strawberry ice cream Afro," she said.

"I've never dyed my hair before," I said.

"It'll look really good on you, I can tell. And we gonna deep condition so your hair stays healthy."

I put my phone on silent and put it away. I looked over at Desi and she was putting her phone away, too. I saw her roll her eyes before she got eye contact with mine.

"Ol' Blackfishing ass. This FAN girl from my Spanish 3 class really just texted me asking if I can cornrow her hair for her for this Megan Thee Stallion show. How do you say 'hell to the naw' in Español? I don't know what's worse, the ones who cake themselves in tacky ass beige foundation or those that seem a little too eager to fade to Blackness like it's the new Balenciagas."

"The thing is they will never get it, really. How it really is to be Black like us."

"It's true. And how even with all of the hard stuff, I wouldn't ever, ever give up being Black," Desi said.

"Nope," I said, then put my head on her shoulder, feeling tingles and sensation on my scalp with each of her breaths. "I love it."

She slid her dark hand over mine and I slid my brown fingers into hers. She let my hand linger there and then squeezed it tighter to let me know my hand could stay, that it belonged in hers. We looked at the intertwined browns of her skin and mine. Through our hands, I felt the energy of her body float into mine.

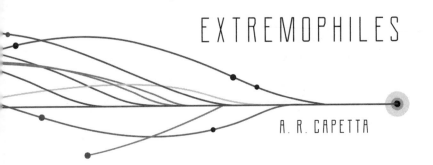

EXTREMOPHILES

A. R. CAPETTA

Testing. Testing.

Conamara to Pwyll. Come in, Pwyll.

If you are reading this message, you've cracked my code. Welcome. First of all, I hope you're not the sort of person who's going to get me in trouble with my dads for junking up these cells with a bunch of base pair sequences that, at first glance, really shouldn't be there—and at second or third glance is an elaborate message to you.

Whoever you may be.

Second! I hope you like long letters, because I am not feeling short-winded these days. I am feeling like there is nowhere in this entire station for my words to go except back down my throat, so I have invented a way to get some of them out and hopefully put some new things in their place, courtesy of whatever is in your brain. I know they used to call this being pen pals back in the ancient days, but I have a bunch of plasmids instead of pens. What if we just call it brain exchange?

I might not be a scientist like most of the humans on Europa, but seeking creative solutions is in my DNA. Just like this message is in the DNA of a fungal cell I messed with. There is a lot of space for junk DNA in even the most basic life-forms. We're pretty messy, even on the tiniest level.

From the mess of my message so far, you must have plucked out the fact that my dads brought me to this icy little moon we call home. One of them is a medic who specializes in space travel. Henry flew to Luna and back to Earth four times before getting this station, which was his dream, partly because it meant he could live on Europa full-time with my other dad. Mack is a gardener. They like to say their jobs are two expressions of the same urge toward life, because they say things like that.

They don't know about this letter. They're too busy with different stages of inertia. Henry is rolling down the hill of a new planting cycle. Mack is sitting very, very still and listening to a lot of Tori Amos. The funny part is that the one who's gardening all day is not technically the gardener! Nobody's had an emergency for a while, and Henry ends up helping in the hothouses when he can't relax, which is always. Mack doesn't seem to mind Henry watering the plants and snipping at the new growth, except when he does. Weird things happen when you let people spend every waking minute together. Some boundaries turn into electric fences. Others just disappear.

I live in the Conamara Chaos, which you know, but I've always wanted to tell someone that I live in the chaos. Except everyone else I know lives here, too, for a grand total of 164 people. Now I've said it to you, so you've already made at least one of my dreams come true.

Tell me about you, new person! What are your dreams? Can I help make at least one of them come true?

From the fact that you are reading this, I will guess that you are probably one of two things. Scientist spouse or scientist spawn. Coding and decoding endless data strings tends to be a task given to these two categories of people. My dads aren't primarily scientists, but they're not *not* scientists. Most people who end up on lifelong missions start out in those sorts of fields, though at some point they have to decide what particular jobs they want, besides spaceperson.

I'm not anything. Not yet. Not quite.

I am hoping you're scientist spawn, merely because that might put us in the same age territory. I'm sixteen years old by Earth standards. Which is still just one year old if you're counting by Jupiter's orbit. When I'm being difficult, my dads call me a Jupiterian infant, and the fight ends.

The most recent fight was yesterday, which is why I'm here, doing the most onerous yet uneventful job in the entire station. It's my punishment. But I'm determined to transform data storage into an adventure.

Will you help me?

With hope,

Lileo

PS If English isn't the language you'd prefer to use for encoding our secret messages, let me know. I only know two others past basic words and phrases, and I picked the one my brain tends to ramble in. But I know that every Europan base has a lot of languages in play. If another is better for you, hopefully I can read it! And if not, I'll find the best translation machine around and also start learning right away!

Hi, Lileo. Message received. English works. To be honest, my best language is math. Please send more words, though. In desperate need of new brain.

X

X,

How can you ask me for more words when you gave me basically none? That was like the asymptote of communications, where I started with this enormous sweep and you did your best to touch absolute zero.

Considering it takes the bunny I 3D printed to hold the cells with the encoded DNA a full month to make it to Pwyll and back, this was anticlimactic, to say the least. And that bunny had to withstand a lot of surface radiation riding in a rover over icy terrain to get to you. It was not an easy journey.

Waiting a month for twenty-six words, no matter how pithy, simply isn't good math. If I don't get at least three whole sentences from you next time, I'm going to cut this off and devote all of my time to my other impossible project.

Still hopeful,

Lileo

Hey, Lileo,

Sorry. It's been hard to talk since I reached the station. It feels like half my words leaked out on the way here. I'm at Pwyll, though I know you know that. Living in an impact crater really shouldn't feel like a metaphor, and yet here we are.

Not scientist spouse or spawn. I science all by myself. I am close to your age, though. They let me come as a sort of last-chance program for social maladapts who test bizarrely well. For some reason, I do better with my peer group when they're four million miles away. Let's hope the Conamara Chaos is far enough to keep you safe from my radioactive levels of awkward.

A few questions . . .

Who is Tori Amos?

Why a bunny? I know it's there because biohybrid data storage is the only way to sidestep how much Jupiter's radiation belt nulls and voids other methods of communication on this moon. But you could have 3D printed any kind of container for the radiosynthetic cells. You chose a bunny, and you made it creepily accurate. It's the uncanny valley of bunnies. It makes me think of the one I had when I was ten. You have a good eye for detail. Especially the whiskers.

What is the other impossible project?

X

Dear X,

I'm going to have to address some things in your last missive out of order because, real-life bunnies? The last time I checked, Atacama was the only base with nonhuman animals of any kind, and honestly, those weren't faring well, except for the penguins. Either Pwyll is running some animal-based experiments I don't know about, or you had a childhood that involved pets. And the only place I know of that has such things is Earth.

EARTH.

Did you come to Europa straight from Earth? How recently? Can you tell from my sudden voracious curiosity that I've never been there? I wasn't even born on Earth. I was born on the flight to Europa. Pure spacebaby. Mack likes to say that I ate stars for breakfast and it made me glittery and restless. I've always wanted to see more of the universe. Any of the universe. This series of little domes is feeling smaller and smaller every day. How many questions can I ask you about Earth without straining the very fabric of our new friendship? Twenty? Thirty?

Answers to your questions . . .

Tori Amos is a singer. She plays the piano and sings, and the notes slip into spaces you didn't know you had. It's funny that you had to come all the way to one of Jupiter's moons to learn about old Earth music. I have lots of books and movies, too, but everything is archival, nothing is synced up with Earth time. I guess I'm living in their past a little bit. But we're also supposed to be helping their future.

We have our own timeline here. Yes, that feels as weird as it sounds.

I chose a bunny because I wanted to imagine softness. Everything on a moon base is hard and sterile, including my pillow.

The other impossible project is why my dads are

so upset right now. I should say mad, but only one of them gets mad. Henry carries around a metric ton of terror about the many ways I could hurt myself. A space medic is basically a walking encyclopedia of possible catastrophes. When I propose doing anything that could cause more harm than a single skinned knee, he converts terror into anger, and he freaks right out. Mack just turns quietly sadder by degrees, which is so much worse.

I definitely knew better, but on my sixteenth birthday, I asked them if I could take a dive. Not in the immersion tanks, a real one. I know you're studying different things on your base, and I'm not sure how much you know about the others, but here at the Conamara Chaos, we're on a spot where the ice shell is thinner—two meters instead of six or seven.

And under that? So much water.

That salty global ocean is right under our feet, and it's calling me, X. I want to go down into the buried sea. I've wanted it for years. I want it so much that I made the mistake of asking my overprotective parents for it. My dads have been letting me train, reluctantly, but that was more of a concession than any sort of permission. They said that we still have another six months or even a year of remote submersible study to go before a human can explore, and even then it won't be me, it'll be some special wreck-diving expert from Earth.

First of all, my moon is not a wreck. Second of all, nobody from Earth knows this place as well as I do. Third, if the whole point is finding life, they really should send me. I'm so desperate to connect with new life-forms that I'm literally sending bunnies into the void.

They said no. Technically, Nia, the dive supervisor, said no, but my dads must have swayed her, because Nia is the one who's been training the official dive team and me in the salt tanks. It helps that she was an Olympic swimmer in another lifetime, back on Earth. Nia knows that you can be a teenager and make things happen. They're not mutually exclusive at all.

When I told my dads that Nia said no, they looked more than relieved. They looked guilty. I got into a real ice storm of an argument with Henry while Mack just frowned at us over a dinner he'd made of vegetables from his gardens and dehydrated protein and Europan salt. It's the only thing that actually comes from here, but we have a lot of it. I hope you like salt, X. Everything is about to get very briny.

I accused my dads of treating my existence like an experiment instead of an actual life.

They said I'm not old enough to understand that I would be risking that actual life if I dived alone into an ancient, ice covered ocean that no human has ever touched or mapped. Mack said that it was all bacteria down there anyway, just a bunch of extremophiles hanging out near hydrothermal vents and in the frigid ice, which we already know from the submersibles.

There's only the tiniest chance of finding anything else.

I said that the life we could find down there was worth any risk.

Which I really do believe. But I didn't tell them the rest. I haven't told anyone this part, because it's a little too much to admit out loud, but I'll say it to you. I believe that there's something more complex and wondrous living in the dark, quiet water beneath our feet. Yes, there are bacteria somewhere other than Earth, and that's a big deal, but maybe everything's not always about Earth. Maybe whether or not we confirm second genesis on Europa isn't even the point. Discoveries are a big deal, but they still center humanity. And I want humanity to get out of its own way. I want to know about so much more than myself.

I believe extremophiles are only the beginning of life on Europa, not the end. There are creatures in that ocean, X. I can sense it somehow, but how do you explain that to a station full of adults who've built their life on the explainable? You show them, right?

So the other impossible project is to get down there somehow.

Now that you're talking to me—really talking—I have hope for that, too.

Your new friend,

Lileo

Hey, Lileo,

I like the sound of your endeavor.

I also like the sound of your dads. I miss my mom way more than I want to admit. You're lucky not to be alone out here, even if it means fighting with people over vegetables and sometimes feeling like they hold you back. I hold myself back enough that I understand the resentment, but at least you get to point it at somebody else, right?

Wow. That sounded bad. But it's too late to unsay it. There's no delete function when you're coding secret messages into DNA.

For that reason and a few others, talking to you feels slightly dangerous. Not exactly like being in a salty ocean that nobody's explored before.

But not *not* like that, either.

And yes, you can ask me about Earth. I go there every night.

The spaceflight to get here took about four years. That's faster than it used to be, and the ships are near luxury compared to some of the older models. I left when I was fourteen. Other people back home were slogging through painful crushes and first jobs and endless academic testing, and I was in space.

I had detached from reality, but in a good way.

I took a lot about that ship for granted, though. It was designed to mimic Earth, from the food to the lights that cycled through our circadian rhythms. I was totally lulled. I thought I'd been living in a new environment, but really it was just an extension of the old one with really amazing views of the stars and a lab that brought actual human tears to my eyes the first time I saw it.

Then I got to Pwyll. The people here don't try to pretend they're on Earth. It's a completely new set of environmental inputs. One of the main things that can happen is this disruption of sleep, it distends and plunges you into deeper REM cycles, basically turning you into a dream machine. I've been here for six months, and I'm still dreaming like that every night. It's so vivid and delicious that I feel like my brain is the kind of dessert they bring to your table and light on fire in front of you.

This is how it starts.

I'm back on Earth, surrounded by animals. Every animal I've ever seen, and every plant, too, grow-ing out of control. The sun is so bright, high-noon-at-the-apex-of-summer bright. I'm in the place where I went to science camp, and the other kids there are wearing camp shirts, which are far too yellow, like the color is a substitute for natural cheerfulness. We were not a cheerful bunch. We were so serious, and all we wanted was to outdo each other. But in my dream, we're all trying to find each other while the animals run and hop and stampede around us, and whenever I find another kid, we hold hands for just a second before the plants get in our way, twisting up from the ground because the soil is so rich and the sun is so bright that they just can't help thriving. The animals run between us. The other kids and I aren't upset when we have to break apart and find each other again, though. We just keep trying to connect for a few seconds. That's the whole point.

Then I wake up, and the sun is so far away that it will never wake me up by rising, and I realize that I'm never going to see a single one of those animals or plants or people ever again.

I'm sorry. I know that describing your dreams is supposedly the worst thing you can do in a new friendship. Dreams are too personal, right? Not in the feelings sense, but in the not-worthy-of-sharing sense. They're just these recalibrations our bodies are doing. They're just overflow valves for our emotions. They're just buckets of associations and metaphors.

I hope I didn't ruin anything between us by being too dreamy.

Ha. You see what I did there?

X

PS Is Lileo short for Galileo? I just put that together.

Dear X,

For a child prodigy, that took you a minute. Yes, my name is Galileo, for all the obvious reasons.

Your dreams sound really intense. I wish I could wander around in them. I wish I could hold hands with all the kids you didn't make friends with at science camp. I wish I could hold your hand, too. As an experiment. And then we could look at the data on what happens after that.

Would you get weird with me? Would I get weird with you? Would it feel totally normal? Would that be the weirdest thing of all?

It's getting weird to think that you have fleshy dimensions I can't see or touch. It's so exciting to discover your words each month and so comfortable to settle into them. I wonder how excited-comfortable we'd be with the rest of each other. Would every-thing automatically seem easy because of our brain exchange? Or is there always a learning curve for bodies? Are you really as awkward as you say when faced with a many-dimensional person?

I'm going to tell you a truth, X. I don't think you and I are like most many-dimensional people, and I'm not saying that to romanticize how weird we both are. This is a deeper biological truth I'm talking about. I think we're like the extremophiles. Made to thrive in unexpected places and impossible conditions. Maybe that's how I know there's something else in the ocean below us. Other people swear it's not conducive to life, to real, complex, interesting, messy life, but they're basing that conjecture on what they already know. You and I know something different.

I'm going to break into the dive room tomorrow and get under the skin of this moon.

I'm going to live your dream, but on Europa.

It's time. Wish me luck.

Heart in my mouth,

Lileo

PS You're not alone out here, you have me. And whatever I find down in the deeps!

Lileo,

Oh shit. I can't believe you're actually doing this. Wait, I can.

Wait, have you already done it?

I feel like I'm living in your past. Like I can't catch up with what you're doing because it already

happened. Or maybe you didn't get into the dive room yet, maybe it's harder than you thought, but I won't know for another month that you're still in a holding pattern. I don't know.

Time feels broken.

I want to tell you about what I saw last night, but that feels slightly broken, too.

My dreams are changing, Lileo. The longer I'm on Europa, the more they twist into something different. Something I never could have anticipated back on Earth. These dreams aren't just friendship killers and metaphor buckets. I think they're a way for my brain to adapt to its new environment.

To tell me the truth about this place, if I'm willing to listen.

We're both looking for truths about Europa in our own extreme ways. Mine involves delving into sleep for sixteen hours a day. Yours involves diving under the ice shell that I'm standing on right now. It makes me feel weirdly connected to you, knowing that you might be down there, under all of our feet.

Did you find anything? I need to know.

X

Lileo,

This month, the 3D-printed object that arrived with radiosynthetic cells inside of it was just a blank-faced cube. No bunnies in sight. No secret message slipped into the junk DNA. I miss your words. I miss digging for every one of your meanings. You're not an experiment to me. Experiments have controls, and there's no control group for talking to you. No way to know what I should expect. Any truth could be revealed at any time.

My turn, I guess.

Did I tell you why I was put on data storage duty in the first place? Weird to haul my brain all the way out to Europa and not use it for something more important, right? But when I first got here, I was a complete washout disaster. They didn't know what to do with me. It wasn't just that I spent most of my time dreaming. When I was awake, I could barely function. I didn't know what to do. I didn't know up from down. Autonomic functions got wobbly and unreliable. Breathing made no sense. I couldn't look out at the rusty bands on the washed-out teal surface of this moon without wanting to throw up. I couldn't wake up without running obsessively through every choice that had brought me here. Not just my choices, either. Choices running back and back for generations. My parents and their parents and everything branching out through different eras of evolution and geological time, until I was in the primordial soup, second-guessing everything.

My supervisors talked about sending me back. Can you imagine? Making it all the way out here only to be sent home? My mom literally sold our house to get me on that spaceship. I was having such a hard time in middle school. I knew the guidance counselor better than I knew anyone in my class. To be fair, Ms. Pike was great. But everyone knew I needed something really different in order to thrive.

And then I got here, and I did the opposite. I anti-thrived. I shattered.

My supervisors stuck me on data storage duty because it cost a lot less money than a return trip to Earth and the last person in this job had broken their wrist. I thought it would be more monotony and claustrophobia, and those things were already breaking me.

All I was supposed to do was comb through the experimental data from the Conamara Chaos to find out if there was anything useful for our own experiments at Pwyll. They put me in a tiny dark room and prepared to forget about me. I braced myself for a brainless, thankless existence. But only a few weeks into encoding and decoding, I saw your words, hidden in endless strings of ATGC.

You surprised the shit out of me, Galileo. And then you kept doing it.

I think your mind is the extreme environment I like best.

Things are different now. I can breathe and eat a whole bowl of pudding in one sitting, and yes, it's salty pudding, and yes, I'm still sleeping a lot, but my dreams feel like a string of secret messages. And when I'm awake, the hours aren't just blank containers. I'm even semi-friends with a few of the younger scientists. I've been given my choice of projects, and I told them I want to study the buried sea. We have a dive site. Did you know that? It's new. I haven't been training like you have, so I don't know if they'll ever clear me for an actual dive. Most of my job is ferreting truth out of numbers. Even when I'm not on data storage duty.

But that's how I know that we're changing incrementally all the time. That's what the other scientists I talk to seem to forget. It's what hit my brain like an asteroid when I first got here. When we step foot on this moon, we're not just studying new life-forms. *We are new life-forms*.

And maybe you've been here long enough to start feeling what else is out there. Your senses are expanding and changing to suit the environment and the input streams, showing you messages that the rest of us don't even know how to decode.

I believe there's something in the buried sea, Lileo. I want to help you find more life. Not so we can say we discovered it, but because connecting is what I'm here to do, even if I couldn't imagine that back when I left Earth. It would have sounded impossible. But a brain exchange through altered DNA traveling across the surface of an icy moon also sounds impossible.

So I'm on the dive site team now. I told my supervisors that I want to keep running data storage, too, of course. They said that the radio has been working really well lately and we might not even need to use the backup data storage system if we can keep it running consistently. The radiation around Jupiter makes satellites pretty much impossible, but I guess they've been working on a point-to-point rocket system that would allow us to send more traditional archives of our data to other bases. No DNA encoding or decoding necessary.

The idea of being cut off from you is really messing with me. I know it's not your job to make me functional, but you're my friend.

I'm worried that if they stop sending the biohybrid data storage units before we talk again, we're screwed. Unless you want to stop talking. Did you not find anything down there in the water, Lileo? Did it make you feel like this connection was a source of false hope?

Or did I do something wrong? That always feels possible. Did I not use enough sentences? I swear I will flood this entire crater with sentences if you write back.

I had another dream last night. For the first time, you were there.

Let me know you're still listening, and I'll tell you all about it.

X

PS I wrote my mom a letter about you. I hope that's okay. It won't reach her for another month. The rockets that take data up to the satellites for transmission back to Earth only leave Pwyll every few weeks. By the time she knows your name, our whole friendship could be a thing of the past. It's a horrible idea, but I'm trying to face it head-on in case I don't hear from you again.

PPS There is always, of course, the slight but non-zero possibility that you made it to down to the buried sea but didn't make it back.

PPPS Even if you're done talking to me, please tell me that's not true.

Lileo? Lileo?
Galileo, are you there?
Testing. Testing.
Pwyll to Conamara. Come in, Conamara.

X,

I'm here. I'm always here. I'm never going to be anywhere but here in the chaos. I'm certainly never going to the buried sea. And you don't need to freak out about keeping in touch with me now that you have your like-minded high-testing friends. You can let go of any hopes you attached to me, okay? I'm nothing special. Being born in the stars and raised on a moon sounds magical, but it doesn't change the fact that I'm just another bored teenager looking for some way to rebel against parents who are making life impossible. It sounds like you're much more likely to live my dream than I am.

Go science yourself. Have an amazing time. I'll be fine.

Lileo

PS Your mom will survive our friendship breakup, I promise. My dads certainly did.

PPS Please describe your dream anyway.

Dear Lileo,

What the hell happened over there?

I'm glad that you're safe and everything, but other than that, I am made of concern.

I am going to distract myself from worrying by telling you about my dream.

It starts like the one I told you about before. There are animals and plants everywhere. Sun pouring all over me. Kids in yellow moving around really

fast, darting like fish. I'm chasing them, playing the same game as usual, but I can't seem to keep up this time. I can't move as fast as everyone else, and the grass keeps getting in my face and tickling my nose. Then I realize the grass isn't grass at all. It's this flowing, fast-growing kelp. And the kids aren't really kids, and they aren't really fish.

And the sunshine isn't sunshine. It's you.

What I mean is, you're there with me, in a dive suit shining this big warm light all over me and everything around me. We're not on Earth. It's shaded into somewhere else, but it feels the same as Earth felt. And there's life everywhere, just as much life as there was on Earth, but it's different.

And then . . . stick with me . . . Galileo shows up. Not you, obviously, because you're already there.

Galileo Galilei.

I don't know that much about what he looked like, so in my dream, he's this medium-old Italian guy with a beard. It's tucked into a dive suit, which looks really uncomfortable. We're the only three people who don't seem able to breathe in this environment. Everybody else is just inhaling cold salty water like it's nothing. And then Galileo looks straight at you and says, "Good job, little fish. All you had to do was be patient."

You two hold hands, and nothing can break you apart.

Then I wake up.

That's all I've got. I'm sorry your dads are mad at me. I'm sorry you haven't gotten to dive yet.

Your

X

My dear X,

Damn your epic dream. It ruined my sulking. It ripped me out of my chilly, dark mood. It even got me to stop listening to Mack's Tori Amos albums. As it turns out, I can't forsake my only friend just to make a dramatic point.

Here's what happened in all of that limbo time when you were waiting to hear from me.

First, Nia caught me breaking into the dive room. I had just gotten the zipper all the way up to my sternum when I heard this horrifying creak of the door. There was nowhere to hide. It's just a lot of freestanding monitoring equipment and thermally regulated dive suits and gear.

So I went down the ladder and waited in the hole in the ice. It's almost two meters deep, tall enough that I could completely disappear unless somebody looked straight down into it. I thought about going into the water, just plunging right in, but I didn't have an oxygen tank. And I didn't really want to die.

I think my dads were worried about that. That

maybe my need to dive was a death wish all dressed up. It's not. It's the exact opposite of that, and if they were paying attention, they'd know it.

So I was down in this ice hole, every inch of my skin coated with shivers under the suit.

And I heard Nia's voice.

"I'm not going to look down there and see if Lileo is attempting a dive. Otherwise, I'll have to put a stop to it and tell Mack and Henry. And I know how hard Lileo has been training and how important this is. So I'll just be right over here monitoring the equipment."

I couldn't believe it. Nia was going to let me dive. She was going to *help* me dive and claim to know nothing about it at the same time. I crept back up and got my oxygen tank on, and she pretended I wasn't even there. It was kind of ridiculous and kind of incredible.

This time, when I went down the ladder, it felt real. I took the last few steps down into the icy, sloshing water. It was running fast, and it nearly swept me away as soon as I put both feet in. It's easy to forget that there are tides under the solid ice. But Jupiter is pulling on its moons really hard all the time. There's so much happening under our surface.

I kept one hand on the last rung of the ladder as the water closed over my head. It was dark, and as soon as I let out all my breath, it was calm. Some people might have freaked out, but I could imagine letting go and living down there.

And then something ripped me right out.

It was my dad. Mack.

He got wet and cold hauling me out of the dive site, and he sat with several blankets wrapped around him, drinking his favorite chamomile blend and scowling at me for about an hour before he talked.

He was finally mad.

First he said he could get Nia fired and sent back to Earth and put on trial for reckless endangerment, and I had to talk him all the way out of that particular hole. Then he said that Henry had found our letters when he was tearing my room apart to see if I was hiding somewhere.

I've been keeping copies of them, X. I hope that's not a violation of your privacy or anything. Well, I've been keeping my decoded versions of your letters, and I've been writing out copies of mine so I have a complete set. Henry read them, muttering parts out loud while I blasted Tori Amos to wash out the sound of his voice.

It was a bad twenty-four hours.

When the day had lapsed, my dads sat me down in our little living room. It's about the size of a walk-in closet on Earth, or so they keep telling me.

Mack took a deep breath and started talking.

This is what he said, more or less, edited by my imperfect memory of a very intense day.

"Our generation grew up in new territory, Lileo. Mack and I were just kids when COVID-19 hit and global pandemics became a reality, and so many people were getting sick, and we all had to cut ourselves off from social contact in a lot of ways. But that isn't really what I want to talk about. This is about what happened later. We made big steps forward in space exploration because suddenly here was this generation who'd grown up with a limited sense of space, an ability to deal with social disconnection. We could exist inside the parameters of extended space voyages in ways that people before us just couldn't. And countries were willing to cooperate on international space exploration in ways they never had before. After so much of the world had shut down, suddenly the universe was opening up. But even growing up the way we did, we couldn't be sure of what it would mean to raise you like this. Sixteen years, no exits. And you're amazing.

"But we still worried that the first time you got a chance to connect with someone outside of Conamara, you wouldn't know how to do it. You'd end up hurting yourself. Or someone else. Social exploration can be as dangerous as scientific exploration. But you've made something beautiful happen with X. We should have trusted you. We have to start trusting you."

"Does that mean you'll let me dive?" I asked before Mack even finished the last syllable of that last word.

"You really think there's life down there, don't you?" Henry said.

They knew that from my letters to you. Henry reading them is still not my favorite thing, but it also gave him a way to connect with me. This current version of me. The one who's sixteen and from a completely different part of the solar system than he is.

"I know there's more," I said. "And X believes me."

Now I know you feel it, too. I didn't say that, because I didn't know it yet.

"Speaking of X . . ." Mack started.

Henry finished his sentence in that eternally coupled manner they have. "We think you did a great job befriending X, but we don't want you to talk again until we know more, okay?"

"More about what?" I asked.

Henry muttered something about catfishing, which I still don't understand at all.

My dads checked up on you and discovered that you are, in fact, eighteen and a recent arrival to Pwyll. They also told me your full name and used some gendered pronouns that must have been in your file, but I won't use those unless you tell me to. I've been told that Earth-born folks can be obsessed with gender and defining and policing it for other people. It's one of the many, many reasons Henry and Mack felt so ready to leave. Henry is trans, which I don't think I told you yet, because it's something I barely think about on a day-to-day basis. When I was little, my dads gave me a lot of space to figure things out and name them for myself, in my own way and my own time. Nobody made choices for me that I had to write over or fight back against to be who I am. Growing up on a tiny moon base comes with restrictions, but there are freedoms that shape everything.

There are also a lot of group decisions that take forever.

The real reason I was gone for so long is that I, uh, got in some trouble for using the data storage module for personal enrichment. I knew I wasn't supposed to add my own messages to the data, not that I ever skimped on the actual experiments. But I was aware that it could go badly, and I just didn't care. I needed to talk to someone.

And then I needed to talk to you.

The board that runs the space station suspended me from the job until they could decide what to do about me going rogue.

Mack had me put on garden duty with him. At

first, I hated the enforced parent-kid time. But then I started to fall in love with the plants. The bunny-soft lettuces and papery garlic and aggressively good-smelling herbs. Even the grass. I would talk to all my seeds and cuttings, sort of the way I talk to you. At first, I couldn't tell if they liked it, or if they even really heard me. Also like with you. But then I could see that they were growing. So I just kept adjusting the sun lamps and digging up more stuff to say.

Mack says that the plants he grows on Europa are already slightly different from the versions back on Earth.

Obviously, the board decided it's okay for me to come back to data storage, but I think they mostly don't care if we carry on like this for a little while longer because, well . . .

They're finalizing the new way to carry data from base to base. Our data storage system is being discontinued in two months. Even if it wasn't, I'm going to be busy. I'm joining the dive team full-time, with Nia and that wreck diver. My dads apologized to Nia for threatening to get her fired with a real Europan feast. They even baked a pie. A very salty pie. And the wreck diver is not so bad, as it turns out. They started diving in the Great Lakes when they were my age, which meant my dads were finally outnumbered in the arguments about whether

or not I could survive. After only a few more auxil-
iary arguments, Mack and Henry said that I can dive
for my seventeenth birthday.

Earth birthday, that is. I'll still be one on
Jupiter.

My dads are only three, though. We're all super
young here.

Love,

Lileo

Dear Lileo,

The version of me who left Earth would have
freaked right out at several points during your last
letter, but I only had a single mild panic attack
when you described getting pulled out of the water,
so I must be evolving. I'm good with keeping things
gender-nonspecific for now. Just to give me some
time to think without all the Earth pressure. Thank
you for asking. And about my name, well, you can call
me whatever. But I do like being your X.

And now I might have the chance to be your
many-dimensional X, too. You know that point-to-
point rocket system that's going to carry experimental data all over Europa? They're also working
on a sort of exchange program from one moon base to
another. I was the first person at Pwyll to put my
name down. I can also un-put it down if that seems

like too much. But if you want me there, I'll be able to watch your dive in real time. I can even hold your hand before you get into that really intense dive suit. If it helps.

We had only two months left when you wrote your last letter, which means this is my last letter to you, and even the idea of seeing you in so many dimensions can't seem to stop me from missing this. Writing to you. I have so much nostalgia for something that hasn't even stopped happening yet.

Is there a scientific term for that?

In order to keep this moment from being the end, and to make this record of our early friendship feel really complete, I'm going to tell you one more dream. The one I had last night, right after I found out that you could be a part of my future, not just my past.

This one doesn't even start on Earth. The creatures don't look like anything I've ever seen. They're so different I don't even know how to categorize them. Some have so many tusks, and others are plants that also seem to be singing, and some are jellied blobs that light up in interesting patterns that I'm sure are messages of some kind.

You're there. I'm there.

The other Galileo went back to Italy and his own time period, I guess?

There's one other thing I have to say, even

though I'm still radioactively awkward about these things.

Here it comes.

Love you, too,

X

Dear X,

By the time you read this, you're going to be packing for the chaos. You'll be less than two days away from meeting me, or at least the parts of me you don't already know. Which is intense, since you already know more parts of me than anyone. It might seem like I'm not scared of anything. As it turns out, meeting the person you're closest to in the entire universe is higher on my personal terror scale than diving into dark frozen water that's literally never been touched by human skin.

But that's only because I really want it to go well.

Once you get here, we'll spend a beautifully synchronized day together before I take my first dive. But for right now, I'm still lagging behind the story, and I have a month until it finally happens. So I want to give you your welcome present a little early.

It's a dream I had. You gave me so many of your dreams, and I never gave one back because mine have traditionally turned out murky and unmemorable. But last night, I had one that must have been snatched from one of your deep REM cycles. You really did exchange part of your brain with mine, didn't you?

Here's how it starts. My dream. The one where I finally go down into the buried sea.

I spend the pre-dive hours with you and my dads, eating sweet potato pancakes made mostly from ingredients that Mack and I grew in the greenhouse. All three of you walk with me to the dive site.

You get really excited about the tech and the dive suit and the setup where you get to watch me. You run around like a kid after too much dessert. You are a science type, after all.

And then you calm down enough to hold my hand. And that calms me down enough to put my dive suit on.

Right before I start climbing down into the ice, Henry tells me the story about how his parents came to the launch of the ship when he left for Europa. They tried to convince him at the very last second to stay, all tear-streaked and horribly sincere. They begged him not to "abandon his birth planet." He promises never to be that dramatic with me. I give him an enormous hug. One for Mack, too.

I save the one for you until I get back. Because I am coming back to you.

Then I'm with Nia and the wreck diver, and we suit up and head down.

The ladder is short, and the water is freezing. Even with an insulated suit. We don't fight it, though. We relax and float with the tide. This tidal energy is what creates enough heat for the ocean to exist below the frozen shell in the first place. It's one of the forces that might be strong enough to create life here, even with the sun so faint and far. The tide is my friend. I let it tug on me and show me where to go.

As soon as it turns gentle, I start to swim down. And I feel something in my head. Not a voice, but as strong and clear as a voice.

Can my senses really be changing, X?

I swim down, because that's what the sense is telling me to do. The dark water swirls around me, and I don't see anything at first, but I feel something. Reaching. It might not even be here right now, the complex life I've been talking about, that you've been dreaming about. What if it's not going to evolve for millions of years? Time is different for us on Europa. Not broken. Bigger.

Maybe what we've both felt is the future, reaching out in all directions until somebody paid attention to it.

Or maybe there's something down there. Right now.

There are lights in the distance. Pinpricks, like stars. Or planets. Or moons. I follow them, because of course I do.

When Galileo first saw the moons of Jupiter, he knew it shifted the whole universe. Away from us at

the center. Toward the possibility of more. All we
had to do was accept that we weren't the only ones
who mattered.

I keep swimming down. I keep reaching.

There are extremophiles down there, hanging out
by the hydrothermal vents, glowing in the dark,
lighting my way.

I breathe in deep, and without speaking a word,
I send a message.

Is there anyone down here?

Galileo to the universe.

Come in, universe.

...Pancakes?

The beast emerges!

Okay, kiddo, today I'll be doing soil samples with the grad students in that area by the old barn.

Can I help with your project?

Not today. Try to relax, at least a little!

si——————lence

Ribbit, ribbit. Coming through.

Climate data trends "very encouraging," says CT Department of Ecological Preservation.

Hi there, what can I get you today?

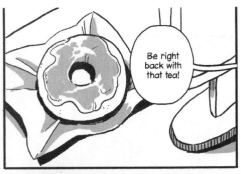

Be right back with that tea!

—the CRYPTID in the woods.

If anything, it's a ghost.

I swear!

I saw it last week!

Don't be stupid, we don't have cryptids up here.

You guys have been watching too much Real Folklore.

Have a nice day!

There's no such thing as ghosts.

There's no such thing as ghosts.

Or cryptids.

SNAP

Keep it together, Astrid.

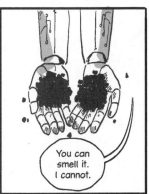

Hey, Dad?

Hm?

Why are all the robots we see now shaped like animals?

Were there ever like, human ones?

Other than in old sci-fi movies, I mean.

When I was very young, there used to be.

A few of them got a little too smart.

They made people nervous.

"Why don't you do some research online?"

WEB ARCHIVE: INTERNATIONAL TREATISE ON AI ETHICS, EFFECTIVE DEC 1, 2320

9:30 PM

10:30 PM

"I am conscious, but not human. Respect that."

11:00 PM

Turing Corp to recall and destroy all helper models after "Jane" tests successfully for conscious thought.

12:00 AM

Atlas to discontinue its custom models after losing lawsuit regarding AI personhood.

1:00 AM

"I know there are only like a handful of conscious robots in the world and they haven't been seen in years BUT— can I marry one?"

Wow. That person's weird.

Next day.

Hey...

My dad says taking a break is okay!

But is it, really?

He says this while doing actual important work!

...

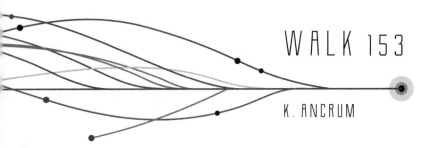

WALK 153

K. ANCRUM

WALK 153

A lot of clients request rain.
I've gotten used to having a wet collar.

"Walker identification: Walker four thirty-five. Location: Chicago. Time: one fifteen a.m. Weather: rainy. You've booked a forty-minute walk. Premium members have recording capabilities. Please press the red button on your remote to record the session. All sessions not recorded at the time of walking can be purchased later for an additional fee. Press play to begin," I said into the headset. I waited for the light on my wristband to go from red to green.

The green light flickered on. I took a deep breath of the humid night air and began to make my way down the street. The camera strapped to my chest jostled a bit with every step, but the watchers like that, I think. It probably makes it feel more like a real walk than watching a nature documentary.

I walked quickly past the residential streets, making my way to a commercial area so the client could see more than just houses. The rainwater splashed over my mask and ran down the sides of the visor, dripping onto my reflective waterproof uniform jacket. They'd thought of everything to make sure the watcher's experience was unimpeded by weather; fog repellant spray had to be applied to the camera lens, and it had its own visor to keep off the rain. But there was a gap between the mask and the back of my jacket collar, and we weren't allowed to wear scarves, so the back of my neck was wet. All service jobs have features like this—small inconveniences and discomforts that showcase the gap between interest in customer care and investment in employee care.

Sentinel was a good company, an altruistic company, even. But it was still a company.

There was an old woman closing up a noodle stand on the corner. She stacked her paper bowls on a cart, then pulled a large tarp over the top of the stand to protect it from the rain. She glanced at me, then did a double take, her wrinkled face breaking into a smile.

"Ah! Sentinel walker!" she said loudly, calling to me from down the street.

This was a problem. We weren't allowed to talk to people while on a job. But the map clearly insisted that I walk down this road, so I wasn't allowed to cross to avoid her, either. I put up a hand in greeting but also waved it in dismissal and began to increase my pace.

"I know you can't stop," she shouted as I approached. "My husband subscribes. He likes to walk around his hometown,

Jeonju-si. I just wanted to say thank you for all your work. Here!"

She shoved her hand in her raincoat pocket and pulled out a small piece of paper. I nodded at her and took it as I sped past.

"Free noodles!" she yelled after me. "Next time, I hope to see your handsome face!"

I looked down at the paper, making sure to keep it out of view of the camera on my chest. It was a coupon for a meal and a drink, handwritten on a piece of receipt paper. Without turning and ruining the progression of the walk, I lifted my arm and waved to her in thanks. I'd never turned down anything anyone had given me. When I first started doing this job at seventeen, an older walker had explained that the gifts weren't really about us at all. Now, after three years as a walker, I understood him perfectly. They were a ritual. An offering.

The best part of the job was this: people understood, when they saw Sentinel walkers, that we couldn't be stopped or bothered and that we were walking for people who couldn't go out or travel. People who watched the world on screens in groups at nursing homes or in the comfort of their bedrooms. People trying to get back to homes miles away or go on vacations they couldn't afford. They weren't afraid of the sabre net masks we wore to obscure our identities or our eerie silence. They gave us gifts and waved hello.

Everyone knows someone who subscribes, a family member or a friend. Not everyone is sick or in need, but many people who subscribe are. People love to see the sky; they love to see the sun. They love to hear the rain splashing on the sidewalks and see kids running in the streets. They love the sounds of cars beeping and birds singing and strangers laughing at a joke as we pass by.

The map insisted that I walk down an alley, cut across into the roundabout with a park, and stand in the middle of it. The cars stopped politely at the crosswalk, and I climbed the side of the grassy hill until the traffic swirled around me. Per the client's request, I slowly turned on the spot in the opposite direction of the flow of traffic. A little girl, up way past her bedtime, stared at me from inside a car, her little hands pressed against the window. I used the zoom on my remote to enhance the view. They blurred children's faces, but clients liked when the camera focused on things that seemed meaningful. A personal touch. After the allotted time, I climbed back down from the roundabout and began picking my way back toward home.

"Walker four thirty-five. Location: Chicago. Time: one fifty-five a.m. Weather: rainy. Thank you for subscribing to Sentinel Walkers; we hope you enjoyed your walk."

The light on my wristband was still green. After a moment, it turned red—the client had signed out of the application. I took off my mask and turned my face up to the sky, letting the droplets hit my cheeks and dampen my hair.

I crept back into the dorms and began silently taking off my gear in the middle of the shared kitchen. Suddenly, the light turned on. I almost dropped my camera harness.

"Bro, it's, like, two a.m. Why are you even awake?" Josh stumbled into the kitchen and opened the fridge. "Haven't you quit that job yet?"

"What? No," I said, gingerly placing the camera on the table. "Why are *you* even awake?"

Josh yawned loudly, not covering his mouth, and sat down at the table, a box of cornflakes and a bowl in his hands. "I have to be at the lab at three. We have some chicken eggs that are about to bust open with bacteria. Science never sleeps, man. Anyway, don't you get tired of the clients yammering in your ear the whole time?"

"They're not allowed to talk to us," I replied. "The only time I've ever heard anything over my headset was during training, when I got yelled at for going off the map's course even though there was construction."

I sat down beside him and started drying off my equipment. I stripped the degraded waterproof layer off the camera and applied a new one, drying the straps of the harness with a paper towel. Josh watched quietly as he ate.

"How long you been doing this, Ezra? You gonna keep with it after you graduate?" Josh asked carefully. "An undergrad philosophy degree might not get you far."

Josh and I were roommates, but we didn't spend a lot of time talking to each other. Our schedules didn't quite align. I was normally in bed when he woke up for work. It was weird to be running into him like this.

"I've been with the company for three years," I replied with a sigh. "It's basically like getting paid for exercising. Sometimes I even listen to audiobooks if the walk is long enough. It's not a bad job."

Josh chewed contemplatively for a while.

"Three years is a long time for someone under twenty. They should give you a raise."

I huffed, winding up the harness straps neatly. "I doubt I'll get one. I don't even have a boss to do yearly reviews or anything. We're all independent contractors, technically."

Josh put his spoon down and looked at me seriously. "You should still try. Don't be afraid to ask for what you deserve."

WALK 156

"Walker identification: Walker four thirty-five. Location: Chicago. Time: three p.m. Weather: sunshine with wind. You've booked a sixty-minute walk. Premium members have recording capabilities. Please press the red button on your remote to record the session. All sessions not recorded at the time of walking can be purchased later for an additional fee. Press play to begin."

The light on my wristband turned green.

It was Wednesday, and the sun was that bright white that lets you know there would be another storm soon. Chicago has the strangest weather. Our seasons don't fade into each other—you wake to them abruptly. Fall lasts forever until you wake to soft snow and biting winds. The snow blankets the city until one day it's forty degrees, the snow melts, and the gutters run in rivers. You wear a jean jacket through spring until one day you leave school and have to carry your jacket home, sweating bullets all the way.

It was spring now, but summer was coming, and I could smell it in the air. I crossed the street, heading to Millennium Park, a large public green space in the exact center of downtown. This client, #5478932, had been popping up often over the last four months. I'd mostly taken them to dense urban areas with lots of people, but this time they were leading me to a more isolated space.

I trailed close to the decorative bushes that bordered the park walkway and brushed my fingers through their leaves. I leaned in close and rubbed a plant.

"Slick with sharp edges," I said quietly. I think #5478932 likes these small touches. You rarely get long-term repeat clients. Premium members tend to just pick whoever's walking in an area they want to see. They don't usually pick a favorite walker. We're functionally the same.

The map on my phone demanded that I turn right and then left, cutting through the park to emerge on the other side of the street, then continue down a narrow path that led to a tiny family bakery. I stood in front of the bakery and looked down at the map. The instructions stopped.

The headset crackled. "Can you go inside, please?"

The voice was soft.

My hands flew to my ears, as if adjusting the headset would change the fact that I was being spoken to through it.

"Excuse me?"

"Can you go inside? They don't let us go in stores. I feel like a ghost looking into every window," the voice said.

"How did you get—you can't be on this channel. How did

you get access to the speech function?" I asked firmly. "This feature is supposed to be used by Sentinel staff only."

I checked my text messages to see if I'd gotten any notifications from the company, but there was nothing.

"It took me so long to figure out how. Please. I haven't been to this bakery in years . . ."

I stood outside silently. The woman behind the counter watched me through the window. It was a Chinese bakery—I had never been to one before. The smell of bread and vegetable oil was very strong, but good.

I sighed sharply. Then I opened my app, pressed the button we'd been told to push when there was a technical difficulty, and jotted down that my headset needed replacing. The app sent an immediate notification that a supervisor would be in contact in one to two business days. Technically, walkers are supposed to just end the walk if something goes wrong. Even if the camera is still on and we are still connected to the client, people rarely want recordings of walks with equipment malfunctions, so tracking tends to end. Which left me and #5478932 together. In silence. Unsupervised.

I put my hand on the door handle and paused for a moment, thinking hard. Then I pushed open the bakery door.

There was no one else inside. It wasn't a prime location for a shop, as it was out of the way of the majority of foot traffic and in the shadow of a large apartment building.

"Hello!" the woman at the counter said. "Fifty percent off buns today."

My heart was racing. This felt extremely illegal.

"The pork buns are good," #5478932 said. "Or at least they were forty years ago. My dad used to take me when I was a little girl . . ." They trailed off longingly.

I crouched down so the display case was visible to the camera.

"What else do you like?" I asked quietly. If they had only one shot at doing something like this, I was going to make sure it was worth it.

"The egg tarts . . . I like mooncakes, too, but they're not in season."

I ordered the pastries, then sat down in the corner, facing the wall. I looked around the restaurant to see if anything inside would provide a visible reflection. There were a lot of small rules for walkers but only a few that resulted in immediate termination. Showing your uncovered face on camera was one of them. This little jaunt might get me a week's suspension, but sitting in front of a window would be much worse.

I lifted my mask just enough that my nose and mouth were free, balancing its weight on my forehead.

The pork bun had soft, tender bread that pulled apart with a bit of bounce. I placed the steaming bun directly in front of the camera so #5478932 could see the detail.

"What does it smell like?" they asked. "I wish I could smell it, too . . ."

"It's . . . uh . . . it smells sweet, a bit oniony. There's sesame oil on it, I think."

"Oh, definitely!" they said, pleased.

I took a bite and immediately understood why they had broken the app to come here.

"This is incredible," I said, my mouth full.

They laughed. "I thought it might be bad to have to listen to someone chew, but honestly, this isn't too terrible. Try the egg tart. It's not as sweet as you'd expect, but it goes well with milk tea."

I gulped down the pork buns, then picked up the egg tart, cracking its golden shell near the camera.

It was a gentle flavor, almost like flan but a bit softer.

"This is . . . this is really great, thank you. Are you not able to eat food like this?" I asked, forgetting myself. "You don't have to tell me any details. Actually, you shouldn't. Don't answer that."

Client #5478932 sighed gently. "No, I can eat this stuff. It's just that this place doesn't do delivery, and I don't have any close friends to pick things up for me. There are other bakeries, but this one is my favorite. The others just aren't the same."

"Oh . . . I'm sorry," I said, my joy at the egg custard deflating a bit. I wished, irrationally, that I could deliver some to them, but caught myself at the last second before I reflexively offered.

"I'm sure there are many people who use Sentinel who have the same problem," they said with a sigh.

"Actually, most people who use the platform don't live where they've requested walkers. It's more . . . unusual to do a walk in your own city," I said, finishing up the tart and glancing back at the display case.

"I can see you checking that out, you know. If you want more, you should get them. Why hold back?"

"I . . . I'm in college. I don't have the budget for it," I admitted.

I heard some rustling and then a ding. "There you go. An extra tip. Have fun, walker," #5478932 said. "We should probably disconnect now. I'm sure if we stay on any longer, management will get suspicious about why you haven't hung up yet."

The line went dead, and the light on my wristband turned red. I took out my phone and swiped to the app, but the resolution was still the same. I swiped to my earnings. Client #5478932 had paid for her session and added a twenty-dollar tip to my account.

I ordered a dozen pork buns to go.

WALK 157

"Have they tried to fix your headset yet?"

"Nice to hear your voice again." I grinned. "Why the sudden interest in parks? I thought you were a city girl."

Client #5478932 let out a surprised peal of laughter. "I haven't been a young girl in decades. But feel free to keep calling me that—flattery will get you everywhere."

The noise from the streets faded into the background as

I approached the bird sanctuary. It was a vast field of wild-flowers and native grasses at the very edge of downtown. The blooms hadn't started growing yet, so the ground was still brown and green, starting to get lush after the snowmelt.

"All the nature walkers in Illinois keep going to the beach and the woods," #5478932 explained. "I don't want to feel like one of those crunchy-granola campers with all their gear. I want to feel like I'm still living in a high-rise and don't own a pair of hiking boots."

"I see. And to answer your question, no, they haven't come by to replace my headset. They have me on premium request only, with a discount rate for not having audio capa-bilities. Since they shut it down remotely, my headset should technically be completely silent," I said, hopping over a puddle of mud.

"Well, with your other clients, it will be," #5478932 said wryly. "Can you walk gently ten feet to the northwest? I think I see a nest."

I couldn't see it yet, but premium viewers had their own zoom capabilities, so that wasn't a surprise. I stepped gently, slightly to the left.

"Stop! You'll step on it! Just . . . just crouch very slowly . . ."

The wild grasses parted to reveal a small clutch of green speckled eggs. I leaned down close, putting my chest as close as possible to the nest so the client had a better view.

"I've never seen something like this in real life before," I said quietly.

"Lots of animals live in the city," #5478932 said. "We're just one. I used to come here during my lunch break. We weren't supposed to leave the main path and go into the sanctuary, but it's such a perfect shortcut to Lake Michigan."

I stood back up, looked out at the gray sky, and took a breath of fresh water-wind. The waves were crashing against the shore, loud enough that #5478932 could probably hear them.

"Do you want to get closer to the beach?" I asked.

Client #5478932 made a small, pained sound. Then there was some rustling and a sharp gasp.

"Are you okay?"

There was a moment of tense silence before #5478932 answered. "I'm as good as I'll ever be. I would like it if we stayed away from the beach. I don't want to see the water; I'll miss it too much."

I turned around so that my camera pointed away from the lake and back toward the city.

"Could . . . could you stay there so I can listen?" #5478932 asked.

I threaded my fingers through some wild grass nearby that had grown up to my waist.

"To the birds?" I asked. "There were more before I got here and tramped around."

"The waves. I don't want to look at them, but they sound . . ."

She trailed off. It was a minute before I realized she wasn't going to continue. So I stood there in the grass for her. I closed my eyes and listened to the water and the wildlife and the traffic and the voices off in the distance, shouting and laughing, and the soft sound of #5478932 breathing and the beep of a machine in her room.

Then I waited, staring at my wristband until green turned to red.

WALK 159

"You really don't go to parties?" #5478932 asked.

"I'm not taking you to a rave," I said firmly. "And no, I want to get all my gen ed classes out of the way, so I'm taking a twenty-one-hour course load and working part-time. I can party in a year and a half."

She sighed dramatically. "Not even a single bar. God, I haven't been in a bar in ages."

"I haven't been in a bar ever. I'm literally not old enough to take you to either of those places."

I could tell she was rolling her eyes at me. "So much for cross-generational friendships."

"Come on, Five. Can't you think of some family-friendly ideas within walking distance?"

"Ugh, fine. Let's go to the zoo."

"But that's, like, a thirty-five-minute walk away!" I exclaimed, looking down at my map in horror. "You only have twenty minutes left."

"I'm adding another forty. Use those young legs and get to marching. Mama wants to see some penguins."

WALK 163

"Strictly speaking, a movie isn't a walk," I whispered. "The screen quality isn't even good from here. You can literally watch a movie at home."

"I don't want to watch a movie at home. I want to watch it with you and get a running commentary," Five said. I could hear her eating popcorn.

"If I don't stop talking, people are going to start looking at me weird," I hissed.

"Then sit in the back," Five replied unsympathetically.

I got up and moved to a back corner seat. The view was even more abysmal than before.

"I don't know why I'm even doing this," I muttered under my breath.

"Because I'm your favorite client and tip fifty percent over what Sentinel suggests." Five laughed. "Consider it an investment. Also, it's fun."

I opened my app and checked the faulty headset status—it still said maintenance pending. It had been almost seven days, and I was still in silent premium mode. Five wasn't the only premium member who bought my walks, but she was definitely my only repeat client. And, honestly, the only client I looked forward to.

"It *is* fun," I admitted. "But the footage from this is going to be absolute garbage. Are you going to rewatch this movie later so you can actually see what's happening?"

Five just laughed.

After the film was over, she bought another twenty minutes to walk me home.

"Movies were more expensive when I was younger," she explained, "and infinitely worse."

"How could they be worse?" I turned down a residential street, and the brightness from the commercial area faded into a dim haze, a thicket of trees casting shadows over the sidewalk. The noise from the main road grew muffled until there was just the suggestion of activity on our periphery.

"Tickets were, like, thirty dollars before they finally capped cinema prices at ten. And god, the remakes and superhero films." Five groaned. "The superhero films were the worst. They weren't bad movies, mind you; they were just so ubiquitous. A new one coming out every three months or so, perfectly curated for consumption. So formulaic, too. You would have loved them."

I huffed with amusement. "Why do you think that?"

Five *hmm*ed. "Ah. People your age love activities that make them feel like they're part of a group. It wasn't about the movies, per se. It was about the culture. The experience of being in a community with specific shared media to argue over and love . . . or hate. The richness of the shared journey."

"Is that what you wanted? To be part of that culture?" I asked tentatively. I could see the dorms a few blocks away, and I slowed my walking, turning down an unnecessary street. We weren't allowed to be in active mode within five hundred feet of our homes for safety reasons.

Five made that noise that let me know her pain was returning. It was a small sound she couldn't quite control, a whimper almost, that caught in her throat and warmed my ears with how terribly human it was.

"Movie theaters are special. They're a form of community unlike any other. Being together but alone, going on a journey that changes us at our core. Being made to cry or gasp with joy in unison, inches apart from one another, but still so far away . . ."

Five stopped talking for a moment.

"It's like this, I think," she finally said.

"This thing we're doing. Against the rules, in the dark," I said, stopping in the middle of the sidewalk.

"Do . . ." Five paused as if she were too nervous to continue her sentence. She gathered more courage and continued, "Do you want—"

"Yes," I said.

Five breathed a sound like a smile. "At least let me get it out first. Do you want to go to dinner?"

"Where?"

"You pick."

"I can't," I said, looking up at the moon in the crisp night sky. "I have to go where you tell me to go. I can't lead, Five. I can only follow."

Five sighed. "Isn't that a terrible thing?"

I swallowed hard.

"I don't want them to fix my headset," I admitted recklessly.

"I'll break the new one," Five replied, and it sounded like a promise.

WALK 167

"It's not a date, Josh. She's, like, sixty-something, I think," I said, pulling on a nice black sweater.

Josh looked back at me dubiously. He was standing in the doorway of my room, cup of coffee in hand, dark bags under his eyes.

"If it's not a date, why are you trying to look nice? She legally cannot even see you." He nodded at my black dress pants and neat Chelsea boots.

"She's taking me to a nice restaurant. Nice places treat you like crap when you don't look like you can afford to eat there," I replied with a scowl. "And it's not a date because it's not romantic. She's just . . ."

Josh waited patiently for me to continue.

"We don't exchange a lot of details, but she's been inside for decades. Maybe more than twenty years. Having these experiences with her means something different than having them with some sorority girl. It's like . . . if you met someone who had developed an allergy to their favorite food, and all you had to do to let them taste it again was clap your hands. Would you do it? Of course you would."

Josh nodded. "I would. But clapping doesn't cost anything. Doing this does. Especially if Sentinel finds out."

I tightened the straps on my harness with a jerk. "It's been almost a month. And to be quite frank with you, having a company be angry at me means so much less than this. It's worth the risk."

I pushed past him roughly and grabbed my camera and mask off the kitchen table.

The restaurant Five had picked was ovo-vegetarian Italian and very busy. The greeter looked surprised to see me with my mask and jacket but honored my request to sit in the corner in the dark, facing a wall.

"I wish you could get a better seat than that," Five said. "It's a part of the experience."

"It's fine, I don't care. What do you think I should order? Anything you've got a hankering to eat?" I asked, tilting my mask up so the bottom of my face was exposed.

"I prepared this time and ordered in!" she exclaimed. "Unlike our last food adventure, this place does deliver. I got a faux lamb lasagna and the deviled egg appetizer with a glass of limoncello."

"Ugh, deviled eggs?" I grimaced. "Gross."

"Deviled eggs aren't gross, kid. They are a refined barbeque picnic tradition," she snapped. But I could hear her grinning. "I could eat a whole dozen of them if I'm not careful."

"Old people food," I muttered. "I'll get the lasagna and the limoncello."

"You can't have limoncello—it's alcohol."

"What does it taste like?" I asked.

She paused for a minute, and I could tell she was thinking. "It tastes like if someone tried to make lemonade using only sugar and the rinds."

"Sounds bad, but here we go."

When the waitress came by, I ordered exactly what she had, deviled eggs and all. They didn't check my ID, which was thrilling. Five scolded me fiercely about it.

"It's been a month since we met," I said, taking a sip of my water to wash down the sharp tang of vodka. "I don't imagine this is going to go unnoticed for much longer. I'm kind of preparing to be fired, to be completely honest."

Five sighed. "I would say I'm sorry, but that would imply regret. I don't *do* regret, walker."

"You're such a weirdo." I laughed. "I don't regret it, either. Otherwise I wouldn't be here. But you should at least pretend to be sorry."

"Pretending is for weak punks," Five scoffed. "And apologies without constructive action are just words. The tip I'll send you after this walk will carry you until you get your next job. It's the least I can do."

I put my hand on my chest and swooned mockingly even though I knew she couldn't see me. "You spoil me."

"You were spoiled before I got here," she muttered. "Eat your food."

"Well," I said, taking a bite of egg and grimacing at the vinegary flavor, "since we're going for broke, do you want to tell me a bit more about yourself?"

"I think the anonymity gives this friendship a little bit

of spice. But I can tell you some things. My favorite color is xanadu. My favorite time of day is early in the morning—"

"When it's quiet and the streets are empty?" I interrupted.

"Exactly. When the birds have finished singing and the sun is just barely out, but it's still so early that you can stand in the middle of the street and no cars will hit you," Five said softly.

"What is your favorite weather?" I asked.

"Windy, but you can't really get that sensation from the walks. I like when the wind is so hard that it almost pushes your legs out from underneath you."

"Or when the wind is warm so you can stand there and just let it whip you around," I continued. "I wish I could take you to a place like that."

"I could pay them to take my bed to Wales and post me up on the top of a hill, but it wouldn't be the same." Five laughed. "The sheets would start whipping around like crazy, and I wouldn't even be able to do anything about it."

I took another sip of limoncello and let it burn all the way down my throat. "It would be like heaven, though. Just quiet and windy with white billowing around you . . ."

"You talk like an English major," she scoffed. "What are you studying?"

"Philosophy," I admitted, and waited for the scorn I knew was coming.

But Five just *hmm*ed contemplatively. "Well," she said, "I guess someone has to. What's your favorite weather?"

"Oh, we're doing me now? Okay. My favorite weather is . . . sun rain."

"That's extremely edgy," Five said immediately.

I groaned. "Please stop making fun of me."

"I will not!" She laughed loudly. "You could stop saying make-fun-of-able things."

I could tell by then that I loved her. It was suddenly incredibly obvious. A feeling like my heart constricting struck the smile from my face. Five was my best friend. She was my best friend, and there was a chance I would never see her again.

"I want to give you something," I said seriously.

"What? Keep it, don't invest your money on me," she said quickly.

"Not like that."

I finished my lasagna and called the waiter to pay the check. Ignoring Five's questions, I rushed out of the restaurant and started down the street. It had been ages since we'd used the map feature on my phone through the app, but we'd headed this way often enough that eventually she caught on.

"You can't go within five hundred feet of your home or it's immediate termination, walker," she said quietly.

"I don't care."

We went farther into the residential area near campus until the only people near us were students. They glanced at me curiously as I strode quickly past them in full gear. I held up my lanyard so security could tell I was a student and wouldn't chase me down. The light outside the dorm suite was out; hopefully Josh would be as well.

I put my hand on the doorknob and turned it.

"Walker," Five said.

I ignored her and rushed through the kitchen and into the bathroom and closed the door behind me. I stood in front of the mirror, my reflection staring back at me: the blank mask and the reflective jacket with the camera strapped to the center.

"I . . . grew up with my grandparents. My parents just weren't around," I said quietly. "In high school, things were pretty okay, but college has been . . . I'm not from around here, and it's been really hard. I was going to quit being a walker when I started college, but when I got here, I just . . . couldn't. It was all I had."

I could hear that Five was still there, breathing quietly, and I could still hear the beep from the machine in her room.

"These have been some of the best weeks I've had in ages, and I know they have been for you, too," I continued. "I know this isn't going to last forever, and I'm not being sentimental about that. I just . . . I can't . . . I feel like I'm so close to knowing you, and this feels like the last part." I took a deep breath. "If I'm never going to see you again, on a random day when I learn that I've been let go, I want you to at least see me before that."

I unbuckled my mask and slid it down.

"Oh," Five gasped softly. "You're such a lovely thing."

Looking at my face through her eyes was . . . so much. I saw myself every day. My hooked nose and messy curls, the zit on the side of my chin and the freckles crowding across my forehead and cheeks. My dark eyebrows and wide-set eyes, tired and unremarkable. I'd never been called a lovely thing before.

"My name is Ezra."

"It's nice to meet you, Ezra," Five said, and my name melted from her mouth to my ears with such joy that I had to close my eyes to really feel it.

"You're so young."

"Yeah," I replied helplessly. "Maybe you can find me one day, and we can really be friends."

"I—"

The line went dead. No breathing, no beeping. Panicked, I looked down at my wristband, and both the red and green lights were off.

"Fuck," I gasped, putting my mask back on quickly.

My phone rang in my pocket, startling me so badly I almost dropped it.

"Hello?"

"Hello, Ezra. This is Jeanette with Sentinel. We received your maintenance request. Management has requested that you visit the home office to pick up your new parts."

I let out a sigh of relief. "Oh, yes. No problem. Give me a second to open the Notes app so I can take down the address."

"Sure. The location is 1 North State Street, Suite 2020. Please arrive promptly at nine a.m. on Saturday morning. You'll need to provide ID at the front desk before they'll let you upstairs."

"Okay, thanks."

"Also, please bring all of your supplies, including your jacket and camera harness. You will also be attending a behavioral review meeting. The meeting should take approximately one hour of your time."

My heart sank so fast I immediately felt nauseated.

"Oh . . . do you . . . know what it's about?" I asked.

"Unfortunately, I do not. I'm just in the customer service department. My notes say administrative behavioral review. Is there anything else you need before I go?"

"No," I whispered.

"Perfect," Jeanette said in a chipper voice. "Have a great rest of your evening."

She hung up. I dropped my mask on the bathroom sink and slid to the floor. I wrapped my arms around my knees and hid my face in the dark.

SATURDAY

I held all my gear in my lap in a tight bundle and jiggled my leg anxiously. The receptionist at Sentinel's home office was friendlier than I'd expected, but it still didn't make me feel comfortable. There was no one else in the lobby but me. The moment I walked through the door, I could tell this wasn't where they handled customer service calls or general supplies. After my panic attack had passed last night, I'd done some research on Glassdoor and learned that they usually mailed new parts to walkers, along with an envelope to send back the broken pieces.

Even being here seemed wrong and uncomfortable, and the granola bar and coffee the receptionist had offered me just exacerbated that.

"Ezra Cohen?"

I looked up. A serious-looking woman with a sharp bob waved me over. I stood, nearly dropping the slippery reflective jacket, and the distaste on her face increased. I followed her through the office, past large glass-walled conference rooms and executive seating areas, to an office with frosted windows. She opened the door and gestured for me to go inside without her, then closed it sharply behind me.

Sixteen pairs of eyes met mine. There was a long table, and six men and two women sat on either side of it. They looked like attorneys, all of them over forty and dressed in expensive-looking suits and dresses. Their expressions ranged from bored to intensely curious, delighted to incandescently furious. At one end of the table was a much older man. My gaze drifted past him to the wall where, to my horror, there were screenshots of my walks.

The projector displayed high-resolution images of the nest and my fingers nearly touching an egg, the penguins at the zoo, the Chinese bakery, the restaurant with my hand around the illegal glass of limoncello. A thousand other places I shouldn't have been, doing things I shouldn't have been doing. And at the very end of the wall, directly behind the oldest man at the table, was a picture of me with my mask off. Staring directly into the camera.

"Please be seated," the old man said.

I stumbled weakly toward the table and put down my gear with what felt like an earth-shattering clatter, then sank into the chair.

"I'm sorry," I blurted.

"I know," the old man replied.

He stood up and walked around the room while we watched him silently. He touched the projection of the nest softly, then turned around.

"Thank you for coming, Mr. Cohen. Your experiences with Sentinel are very valuable to us, and I'd like to ask you a few questions about it, if that's all right?"

"Okay." I looked anxiously at the man sitting next to me, but he seemed to be the angriest at the table and turned his chair away from me abruptly.

"Was the relationship with your client positively or negatively impacted by their ability to choose the same walker repeatedly with no restrictions?" the old man asked.

"I . . . positively? I didn't really notice anything bad about that feature of the platform for the last three years. But it definitely helps when I know what the client would want to see."

The old man nodded, then returned to his seat and picked up a sheet of paper.

"We noticed that you've always taken care to zoom in on particular things and vary your walk speed often, even though it's suggested that walkers maintain their pace. What was your reasoning behind this?"

"I want to make them feel like actual walks. My ratings increased when I started doing it because people who subscribe don't want to feel like they're just watching TV—they want to feel like they're really going somewhere."

"Exactly!" one of the women at the table said with extreme exasperation.

"Jordan." The old man held up a hand to quiet her, then

continued. "Finally, Ezra, why do you think your relationship with your client progressed so quickly?"

"She's just . . . really cool," I said. This was rapidly becoming humiliating.

"Can you please elaborate on that? We need to understand more about the social development in your own words. We've seen your footage, but that doesn't tell us what you were thinking or any of your motivations."

"He doesn't think you have a crush on her," a patient-looking man added. "We're just seeking more experiential data."

I closed my eyes and willed my face to get less red.

"It's . . . I wanted to work for you guys because I spent a few months in the hospital as a kid and got used to watching walks on TV. It wasn't even the most basic subscription. But it helped . . . even when nothing else did. And I started thinking about how much I would like to see things that the public broadcasts would never show us.

"Five, she . . . she still wants to go places she used to go but can't anymore. She doesn't want to walk past stores—she wants to go inside them. She doesn't want to brush past people; she wants eye contact," I said firmly, starting to get heated. "And I don't want to be rude, but my job here isn't worth more to me than what I did. Even if it was wrong. I get that the rules you have are safety measures, but I just . . . feel like this app could be better if you stopped thinking of your subscribers as people tuning in to a channel. Or . . . or . . . if you maybe thought of your walkers as companions, connections between us—I mean *them*—would be faster."

"Like your connection was fast," the old man said pointedly.

I scowled. "If I'm fired, can I just go home now?"

He gently placed the piece of paper he was holding onto the table.

"My name is Hideki Shimomura, and I'm the founder of this company," he said simply. "The rest of the staff at this meeting is our product development team, legal counsel, and heads of customer service. You're not fired, Mr. Cohen. This is a product development meeting."

He stood and began to walk the perimeter of the room, looking at the images on the wall.

"I initially developed this product to suit the needs of my daughter, who has difficulty with mobility. I built the first harness and sewed the first reflective jacket. I developed the rudimentary phone application and mapping service. I walked for her for fifteen years before I was able to get investors for this company. I understand.

"When the application first became available to the public ten years ago, there were some difficulties, and many of the features had to be adjusted for the safety of both the walkers and the clients. We've been having an argument about increasing personalization, but it's difficult to test things like this in an organic way. The discussion had been shelved for over a year when your maintenance request came through.

"Your headset isn't broken, by the way," Hideki said with a soft smile. "Your client hacked the back end of the app, located your employee code, created a copycat Sentinel staff

ID, and patched in through the company's locked audio channel. She really is a firecracker."

"Why didn't you shut it down, then?" I asked.

The patient man who'd asked about data spoke up. "It's difficult to replicate social connections in artificial environments because people don't act the way they would normally act when they know they're being watched. So we could either remove capabilities on her end or watch and wait to see what would happen. If anything . . . inappropriate began, we could immediately shut it down, the way we did when you showed your face. That was a safety measure."

"Thank you, Theodore," Mr. Shimomura said. "And thank you to everyone else, but I would like to be alone with Mr. Cohen for a moment. We will regroup at three p.m. Jeanette, please submit the minutes to the board and draft a preliminary schedule for product development meetings over the next few weeks."

All of the staff at the table rose and packed up their things. Mr. Shimomura sat down in the chair that the furious man had vacated and waited for the door to close behind the last person.

"Your client sent you a tip through the app right after we closed your connection. Payments sent to terminated or suspended accounts generally rebound, but we caught this for you," he said. "We weren't sure whether you would accept our offer to continue to walk for us, so we processed the payment as a check."

He slid a white envelope across the table.

"She said that she would take care of you if you were fired."

I opened the envelope and, to my shock, slid out a check for fifteen thousand dollars. The name on the check had been covered with a small piece of painter's tape.

I touched the tape and looked up at Mr. Shimomura.

"It didn't feel . . . respectful . . . to share her name with you without her permission," he said. "If you would like to continue walking for Sentinel and sharing your data with us, it would be an immense benefit to us. We'll be upgrading a few other popular walkers to assist with native testing as well. It would be the same pay rate, but your profile would be updated with a prototype two-way communication feature that would allow company-approved direct contact."

I wanted to laugh. The same pay rate. Josh would be thrilled to learn he was right. A company is always a company, I guess.

Mr. Shimomura stood. "Take a minute to think about it. When you're ready, the receptionist at the front desk will help you with your paperwork."

He put a gnarled hand on my shoulder and gave it a warm squeeze, then left the room, closing the door gently behind him.

WALK 171

"Where are we going tonight, Five?"

"You choose this time."

I laughed. "You spoil me. Do . . . uh . . ." I paused and then took a deep breath. "Do you mind if I take you to the lake?"

"I told you Ezra, I don't want—"

"We can face it at the same time," I said, tilting my head back to look at the sky. "I want to see the waves through your eyes."

"Stop being a smooth talker before they shut your app down. No flirting," Five snapped.

"Come on, old lady. You don't have to swim. You don't have to put on sunblock. You don't even have to get grit between your toes."

"Those are the best parts." Five sighed.

"Then turn off your video, and I'll read to you when we get there. It will be like before, and you can just listen."

The waves were dark when we got there, and the wind was strong. The spray splashed against the toes of my sneakers and dampened my face.

"Are you listening?" I asked.

"And looking, too," Five replied.

"Brave girl."

"Ezra?"

"Yeah, Serefina?"

"Thank you."

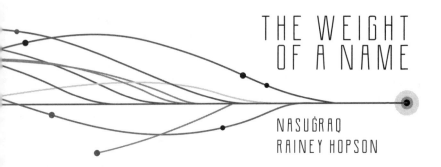

THE WEIGHT OF A NAME

NASUĜRAQ RAINEY HOPSON

T H E best part of visiting the Center was that people weren't allowed to talk to you.

It was customary to leave a Visitor to wander around the vast warehouse alone with their thoughts and decisions. Our culture was sometimes overwhelmingly interactive, with polite words and almost constant social functions, so I treasured these visits for the peace and quiet they gave me. Of course, getting familiar with the Gifts was also fun.

"Allu Saakli, your allotted time is almost done. Please make your way to the front of the building," a woman's voice said quietly from my wristband in an official tone. I tilted my head at the Gift in front of me, a worn metal spoon, probably made from stainless steel. No. This one didn't seem like a fit for me, either.

Does anyone feel connected to a spoon, though?

The Center warehouse was vast, several stories of small, intimate rooms filled with thousands of individual items placed carefully on plain white pedestals of varying heights.

There was just enough room around each item for a couple of people to walk around them comfortably. The items varied beyond imagination. You could find a gold nugget necklace studded with nephrite jade sitting next to a precontact Ipiutak obsidian knife. A shiny new black air-state hard drive next to a yellowing lace handkerchief embroidered with delicate blue forget-me-nots. Items from every age and time in recent history. The items were not arranged in any logical fashion. When one was taken, it was simply replaced with another. Here and there, you would see an empty pedestal waiting for a new item.

Each was in essence only a symbol for what it represented. The gold and nephrite jade necklace could represent a sum of money or an acre of land, or even just be the necklace itself. You never knew what an item truly represented till you chose it on your Name Day, the day you were introduced to the Real People as an adult. This was the only cultural ceremony that was shared with the community instead of just close family, so it was always a big event. Family came from neighboring villages to partake in the feast and debate about what item the young adult would pick and whether or not they would get what they wanted. The crowd always looked forward to the revealing of the Gift. The longer I thought about it, the heavier the decision felt.

Your Name Day was celebrated the day after your eighteenth birthday. The Tribe and People acknowledged that you had become an adult. Your Name was chosen and given to you by the Elders. A Name was more than just a legal identity; it was a chance to reincarnate a part of someone's soul, to bring back someone who had been valued. All of the Gift items and Names were donated by people upon their deaths.

My wristband chirped, notifying me that I had only a few more minutes before the next person would enter the building, then chirped again, this time in question mode. I raised it to my lips and whispered into the receiver, "Schedule another hour as available." It clicked back twice in recognition of my command.

I made my way slowly to the front entrance, taking my time, dragging my feet on the worn neutral beige floor in a steady rhythm. I hadn't yet found an item that spoke to me, and it was starting to get worrisome. My Name Day was a month away, and I didn't want to pick just any old Gift. I wanted to have a connection to it. I had a cousin who had picked the most expensive thing she could find—a pile of gold nuggets that were dark and dusty with age—thinking she would inherit money or at least extra shares in the Corporation. But it was later revealed to be fool's gold. An Elder met with the family after the ceremony and presented them with an old gas-powered car whose former owner had apparently called it "the gold nugget." My cousin was disappointed, to say the least. I just wanted my Gift to *mean* something.

Approaching the entrance, I pulled my light jacket out from my pocket and fluffed it a bit before sliding it on. I could barely feel the silky-smooth garment on my skin. I paused for a minute and whispered under my breath the words that would trigger a temperature adjustment in my body via bio-feedback, and I felt my veins dilate and my skin flush with heat. I tapped the thick glass door at the entrance; it gave way silently in a smooth motion, and I was immediately embraced by the stinging cold outside. I paused to let the goose bumps subside, relaxing my breathing.

As I began walking toward the Port, I looked back at the behemoth cave that was the Center. From a distance, it looked like nothing more than a lump of ice and rock with a small, protected entrance protruding from the base that blocked most of the wind. But inside were all the treasures our Tribe had held dear for the last couple hundred years, a monument to our culture and resilience.

Filled to the brim with wondrous items, and yet I was unable to choose a Gift. *Why am I hesitating?* I imagined all of the items as arms reaching out to me from the past, some with love, some with fear, and some with hope. A connection to all the people who'd come before. But I had always felt untied to any of them, like a kite with no string.

Why is this so hard? Is there something wrong with me?

I frowned and jogged a bit with my head down, trying to banish the negative thoughts. In the event that I did not choose a Gift, my parent or guardian would choose for me, which meant that my aunt Beck would pick one. My aaka had passed away when I was six, and my birth father was an on-again-off-again presence in my life, as unstable as green ice. He was consumed with his own trauma and had long ago stopped seeing me as his responsibility. Aunt Beck, my mother's oldest sister, had stepped in, and with her wide shoulders and quiet steadiness, she was a rock in the storm of my life. She didn't have kids of her own and was easily overwhelmed by all of this stuff. She would not be happy with me at all if she had to choose my Gift for me.

There was nothing worse than an angry rock. She tended to stay angry for a very long time.

The Port building appeared as I turned a corner, a wide block of pale peach with large, glistening, slightly tinted windows facing the street. A deep humming emanated from the building, a sound you could feel in your bones.

I touched the glass door, and it silently opened. The smell of spent fuel and burnt coffee greeted me. I walked up to the girl behind the counter and flashed my wristband over the sensor pad in front of her. She smiled an empty smile at my right shoulder and nodded. I had about fifteen minutes before my flight, and there was no one else in the low-ceilinged waiting room. I found a comfy chair in the back, placed my wrist com on the wall to charge, and pulled out my Synth-Interface tablet. Tapping the screen lit my little corner with a soft cream light. Immediately, my start page filled with talking heads, overexaggerated neon personalities repeating news summaries about the "New World" and rumors of colonization. Before I could dismiss the news rollouts, my screen was suddenly filled with Aunt Beck's wide brown face. Her eyebrows were raised high in a question. I squished my nose in a silent no. She responded by rolling her eyes, and her face disappeared again. Silent communication at its finest.

Text scrolled across the screen: *Be ready, Elder Uali is here to discuss your Gift for some reason.*

A heavy groaning sigh escaped before I could stop it. The counter girl glanced in my direction. My hand moved quickly in our sign language: *sorry.* She shrugged slightly.

Huh. An Elder. That was unusual. Elders only showed up when things were bad and they needed to intervene or if there was something major happening. Was the fact that I hadn't chosen a Gift so close to my Name Day that bad? I would find out soon enough. I clicked through the other notifications on the screen and found nothing else of interest. Worry wormed its way into my chest and grew every time I noticed it.

The flight to my home village was short and uneventful. I was the only person on the transport, surrounded by crates full of vital supplies like fresh produce and parts for a thermal power turbine. The pilot was nice enough and let me sit next to him in the cockpit to get a better view. I think his name was Stin, a short, stocky Englee man who used basic hand language but avoided speaking. I could tell he was used to dealing with our cultural differences but hadn't learned more than was necessary. He seemed like a nice guy, nice in that he didn't have that sneer on his face that so many outsiders did, like they knew something we didn't.

The weather was calm and bright, and the humming of the magnetic drive of the transport vehicle eventually lulled me into a drowsy half sleep. When we landed, I was surprised to see Nuvu waiting for me at the airstrip. His long, unruly dark hair floated around his head in an annoying mess. With his lanky height, he looked like a poor excuse for a willow bush. He was my first cousin by blood and my closest friend, more like a sibling.

I departed the transport vehicle and made my way over to Nuvu, his hands moving quickly in our childhood sign language that no one else could understand, a type of shorthand:

bad, heads up, I don't know. I smiled in his direction, trying to project confidence I didn't feel. He didn't smile back as we walked toward my home.

His long legs moved quickly over the icy surface of the road, and my shorter legs moved faster to keep up with him. He usually slowed his pace to match mine. The worry in my chest moved down into my stomach, and I was glad I hadn't eaten lunch yet.

Nuvu didn't say anything, just walked, stopping here and there for me to catch up. He pulled his hood up over his cloud of hair. Today he wore his favorite jacket, made by his mother—it was pale blue with his family's design carefully sewn into the hem of the lightweight garment. His qupak featured a line of stylized foxes stitched in black and white. I unconsciously tugged down the sides of my own parka, aware once again of the missing qupak that should've been stitched there. The qupak my mother would have made for me if she had been alive. She wore grayling on her parka trim, and I had always wondered if I would have had grayling, too. They were known for their fighting spirit.

Nuvu's eyes flicked in my direction every once in a while, which meant he was *really* worried. Did he think I was in trouble? I knew having an Elder come to talk to you wasn't always a good sign. It wasn't always a bad sign, either. Sometimes they came over if your parents couldn't get through to you about your bad behavior, but not picking your Gift in a timely manner was not an offense. More of an embarrassment, really. It hardly warranted a visit from an Elder. No. It had to be about something a little more serious. With that thought, my palms began to sweat, and I flexed them open and closed to dry them a bit.

Allu, you got this. Whatever this *is. You got it.* I tried my best to banish the anxiety with manufactured bravery.

The pale-hued earthen house that was my home came into view. A small personal vehicle was parked outside. The dark green paint on it was new. Everyone knew which Elder rode that vehicle. Green was her favorite color. Some of the other Elders called it garish, too bright of a color for a dignified person. Everyone referred to Elder Uali as "The Hammer." She was usually sent to get a certain result, and she wasn't very gentle in how she went about doing it. She had also known my family for a few generations—she was my great-aunt or something—and was usually the Elder who presided over our family ceremonies. But we had never actually sat and talked face-to-face before. When she taught us younger people, she preferred to teach to groups instead of individuals.

When we arrived at the door, Nuvu's hand flickered *good luck*, and he walked away toward his own house, leaving me on my own to deal with whatever was going to come out of this meeting. I took a deep breath, wiped my hands on my jacket again, and tapped the door, blinking away the sudden tears as the pressure adjusted in the arctic entryway and warm air hit my face.

Our home wasn't very fancy; a lot of the things we owned were old, but everything worked smoothly. Aunt Beck had instilled in us our duty to care for our home, so if something did break or needed a new paint job or leaked, it usually didn't stay that way for long. The kanitchuck of our house was clean and neat but filled to the top with various outerwear and clothes hanging on the walls. Footwear neatly lined the floor, clean of dust and ready for use. I slipped off my jacket and boots and put them away in their respective places, then whispered the aki—the word that would reverse the change in my body chemistry. Immediately, goose bumps spread across my skin as the lingering cold from outside affected my body. I pulled down one of my sweaters hanging nearby, the thick gray material soft and worn and stretched out in all the right places. Aunt Beck kept the temperature pretty low in the home; she believed it made us healthier. Personally, I thought it was just because she loved wearing bulky sweaters. Ugly bulky sweaters.

Emerging out of the small arctic entry and into the main room, I was greeted by an odd scene: Elder Uali sat in the "good" chair, its soft, deep upholstery holding her frail body like a plump hand cupping a tiny, fragile baby bird. She was so small that her feet didn't even touch the ground—they just kind of floated in the air in front of her in a very undignified way. Her toes pointed at the ceiling. She had a sharp, birdlike face, and her gray hair was pulled back so tightly into a bun that it shined in the dim light of the room. She wore no jewelry or embellishments, which was odd for a woman of her stature and age. Usually, older women loved wearing heavy bracelets and necklaces of ancient ivory or gold, passed down from generation to generation. The only obvious nod to vanity was her atigluk, a short traditional dress shirt with a hood and deep half-moon pockets in the front. It was a vibrant green that shimmered opalescent in the light when she moved. Her dark, glittering eyes darted to me as I made my way closer, the movement adding to her birdlike quality. I looked down at the floor, nodding in greeting.

Aunt Beck was sitting cross-legged on the floor in front of her; she was old-school like that, even though most Elders were fine with younger people sitting in chairs. Today Aunt Beck was wearing a dark blue wool sweater flecked with bright orange and green spots, the thick material making her look wider than she actually was and the colors clashing with her olive skin. I didn't even know where you could buy such an ugly sweater.

I nodded at my aunt, plopped down in front of Elder Uali on the floor, and tucked my feet under me; a little bit of deference never hurt anyone. *See? I'm harmless.*

I waited.

Elder Uali spoke first. Her voice was deep but papery thin. "I'm going to cut to the chase, Allu—I don't like messin' around with speeches and all that. I was sent here to ask you to consider something, a request. It is an odd request, but hear me out. First, I have to say that you're not in trouble, and if you decline, you won't be in trouble."

I tilted my head up and glanced at her face. Her forehead was full of wrinkles as she examined my expression. I nodded and dropped my gaze to my lap, focusing on her words. For some reason, her saying I was not in trouble made me *feel* like I was in trouble.

"As you know, they are sending the first colonies to the New World." Yes, everyone knew about the New World. It had been the dominant topic of every single news report for the past five years; all the talking heads in the media ran with the story nonstop. After hundreds of years of searching deep space, scientists had found a habitable planet only a few light-years away. A ship full of colonizers was being sent to test whether or not humans could survive there. Despite this being the biggest news in all of humankind, the public knew very little about the whole thing. The government was keeping everything as quiet as possible. Some people said that what they knew would cause wars between countries. Some said it was all just a big hoax, that this planet didn't really exist, and that they were feeding news to the population in small doses to inspire tiny little pieces of hope. Some, like myself, really didn't care, and why would I? That world was even farther from us than all the other human beings on this planet. The Arctic is an isolated place.

"Well, it turns out that this planet is . . . cold. Cold like our Nuna. Our lands. It's still habitable, but they'll need to seed the planet with animals and plants that can live there. They have asked for our help, panigaa. They are looking for biological material of ancient frozen animals; they will use the DNA to engineer animals that will better survive there. They need our help finding it. They have other sources of information across the Arctic, but they got wind of something that we have, and they want it."

She waved her hand in the air, as if to wipe away the last of her words, like she wished they hadn't come out of her mouth. I frowned. There was only one thing that would make her feel like that.

"In exchange for what, Elder Uali? What would our people gain from that deal?"

She pinched her lips and again wiped her hand across the air. "We would gain some things here. We would get some land back; we would get some money." She looked me in the eyes then so that I could read the emotion there as she said the next words. "But most importantly, Allu, we would be promised part of that planet. We would get a say in what happens to it. We would get to choose a large portion of the land and resources out there. They *need* us, Allu." The emotion in her eyes was powerful; I could see a pain deep down, rising to touch the surface and almost breaking through. She smiled a little, and it wasn't a friendly smile.

I heard my aunt suck air through her teeth and let my gaze drop to the floor again. I let Elder Uali's words sink into my brain a little. They needed us. How ironic that our government needed us after trying to eradicate us so many times. Even now, we fought to retain control of our lands, inch by inch, mile by mile. Excitement about this news made its way through my mind, but with it came the dark hand of fear.

I don't like where this is going.

Aunt Beck leaned forward, and the sound of her ugly sweater rubbing against itself filled the silence. "What does this have to do with Allu?" Her voice was too loud by the end of her sentence.

Elder Uali picked at a nail, pretending to remove a piece of imaginary dirt before answering.

"Well, that is the thing. Allu is being involved because she has not chosen a Gift yet, and she has a tie with a Gift, so she should get first say." She stared at the wall, giving us some privacy as we heard her next words. "They need a specific Gift from our vaults. Your aaka—your mother—donated a Gift before she passed. It is a set of journals. It is a collection of knowledge; she was a very brilliant woman, you know. She knew these lands better than most. She recorded everything. We do not know many details about the journals' contents, but the government is very interested in them. We are breaking from tradition. You are next of kin, and in older times you would have inherited the journals. So we are involving you and your family, as seems only fair. The journals would be yours if you chose them, of course, and you could decide what to do with them. But this is an opportunity, panigaa."

I looked at my aunt's face, her normally sun-kissed skin pale. Her lips were pressed tightly together. Any mention of my mother left her raw to the world. I felt my own grief scratch at the surface of the walls.

The Elder began scooting forward in the chair, swinging her feet to try to extract herself from its grasp. I got up and offered her my hand so that she could pull herself up. Her hand was dry and cold, and I could feel the bones near the skin. When she stood up, she huffed a bit and smoothed the front of her dress shirt, which made it shimmer brightly.

"I will let you decide, ami? I will need a response soon. A couple of days at most. Otherwise, they will move on to other means of finding these frozen fossils. Please don't spread this word too far. Don't want the crazy news people invading our villages." She shuffled toward the kanitchuck and in a few moments was gone.

I turned to my aunt, but she stood up quickly, ending any type of conversation. She rummaged under the sink and pulled out a spray bottle filled with bright blue liquid and a thick white rag. I sighed. When I'd first moved in, she'd made a rule: when she is cleaning, she needs to think, and I can't talk to her. I watched for a moment as she moved from cupboard to cupboard, first spraying down surfaces and then wiping them.

I walked to my bedroom at the back of the house, letting the words of Elder Uali bounce around in my head. My mother's journals. I had a vague recollection of seeing books when I was young—my mother was odd about old tech like that. She had joked that she'd been born in the wrong generation. How come no one had ever mentioned them before this? Growing up, I'd heard hundreds of stories about my mother; it was practically a ritual. We spoke of the dead often, keeping their memories alive. And I could not remember journals ever being mentioned. She was a Kukiḷukti—a traveler, a jack-of-all-trades in the wilderness—and she took on whatever job was needed and was paying: trapper, scientist escort, sample collector, photographer, animal counter. Not many Englee were allowed into the vast lands that belonged to our People, so her talents were always needed.

I softly closed the door to my bedroom and plopped down onto the bed. I stared at my hands as I rubbed them together. They were damp with nervous sweat. I winced as I realized that Uali must have felt the dampness when I'd helped her out of her chair. How embarrassing. I glanced at the photo of my mother that I kept next to my bed. She was smiling, her hair a halo of mess around her head as she stared off camera at someone.

Aaka, I wish you were here to tell me what to do. I wish someone *were here to tell me what to do.*

I pulled my legs onto the bed, hugging them to my chest, trying to figure out all my feelings. They were tangled like her hair.

My wristband tapped my skin gently, alerting me to a call. I recognized the caller and accepted. Nuvu's face filled the space in front of me. He pulled back from the screen as I explained to him what had just happened. He made the hand sign for *eekanee,* which meant "scary" or "caution." I nodded in agreement.

"Remember all the stories about Raven, Tulugaq?" he said. "Remember what they say about him? Englee always wonder why we are so suspicious of the Raven spirit. He gives us lots of useful things. 'Why call him a trickster?' they ask us." He smiled a tight little smile. "You know what I tell them? I tell them it's because you never know what you're going to get from Raven. Could be good, could be bad. In the end, Tulugaq does what is best for himself. And sometimes Raven doesn't even know what he is going to do. And that's dangerous. Englee are like that, too, in a way. Trusting them too much might get you something good, but sometimes . . . not." I nodded, my hands moving in sign: *confused, worried.*

"What do you think my mother would want?" I asked him. He shrugged. "What if I make the wrong decision, Nuvu? What if I am wrong?"

His eyes filled with sympathy, but he didn't give me an answer.

Later that evening, I wrote a quick note and sent it to the private missive address Uali had provided me. I fell asleep quickly and dreamed about Raven, his black feathered parka a stark contrast to the diamond he held out toward me. In my dream, I reached for it, but my hand was ghostlike and pale.

Normally during a Name Day celebration, there would be all types of excitement to look forward to. A feast prepared days ahead of time. Some singing and dancing, stories that started with "when you were young" and usually ended in laughter, all of it working to connect the newly declared adult to the community. The Gift itself connected you to the past, everything else connected you to the now and to the future. And thus, you were anchored in time.

But this time, there were no celebrations, no community hall filled with a mouthwatering cacophony of food. No walls echoing with laughter and stories. No. They would have to come later, Aunt Beck said. Once I had agreed to be part of this deal, the government had asked permission to move up my Name Day so that they could start tracking down what they were looking for. And we had agreed—for a small amount of additional land, of course.

The gray box measured about a foot and a half square. It sat innocently enough on the plain white pillar in front of me. I reached out a hand and was just about to brush the surface with my fingertips to see if it had dust, but a slim brown hand stopped me.

"Allu, you cannot touch the Gift until it becomes official."

I nodded, cheeks warming with embarrassment as I tucked my hand back behind me. The Inuit woman who'd stopped me from touching the box tapped away at the slim transparent interface screen that glowed softly in her hands, a frown on her dark face. Her name was Bett, and she was a Qaunaksri: she managed the Gifts and was charged with taking care of the items that were housed here. She was also charged with releasing the gifts to the Name Day recipients.

Two other officials stood around the box with me, along with Aunt Beck. They were Englee—one was probably a woman and the other probably a man, judging by the difference in height. They hadn't introduced themselves to us and had already been standing there when we'd arrived. It was hard to tell much about them, because their clothes were so bulky and thick that it hid their shapes, and their heads were covered by cowls. They both wore wide eye coverings that protected them from the glare of the sun on the ice; even though they really didn't need them indoors, they hadn't taken them off. They didn't say anything, only nodded once in a while. Judging by the official-looking badges on their coats and the stiff newness of their clothes, I assumed they were here to represent the government.

The soft sound of shuffling came from behind me, and I turned to see Elder Uali making her way to the podium. She waved a hand in dismissal as I glanced around for a seat for her. Today, she wore an olive-green atigi that almost reached the floor. The length was more formal, but the drab color was unusual for her.

It looks like something you would wear for a funeral, I thought, then wished I hadn't.

"Make it quick, shall we?" she grunted at the two Englee people, eyebrows raised in a question. Aunt Beck shrugged slightly. She had barely said anything at all since Elder Uali's visit the other day. When we had gotten a moment to talk about the situation, she had placed her hand on my shoulder and told me that she trusted my decision. She loved me and fed me and kept me out of the government childcare system, but she had always been at a loss for how to parent me.

Bett stepped forward and ran her hand along the edge of the pedestal where the box sat. There was a faint hum, answered by a click from Bett's official-looking wristband. The box shimmered for a moment as whatever coating was protecting it disappeared. She swung toward me, her hand on the screen of her tablet.

"Allu Saakli, daughter of Hera Saakli, daughter of Tom Burmen, granddaughter of Avu Saakli and George Saakli, granddaughter of Joyce Grison and Tom Burmen Sr. Is this your chosen Gift for your Name Day?"

The abrupt official tone of her voice and the sudden attention of everyone in the room gave me pause. I nodded, then cleared my throat, trying to tamp down the sudden anxiety that ran around my stomach like panicking lemmings. "Yes."

"Place your palm on the reader and repeat your full name for the record, please. Then the item will be officially yours."

The screen of the reader was cool to the touch, and I felt

it shift beneath my fingers. "Allu Joyce Saakli," I said, my voice a whisper.

Bett stepped back, a small, hesitant smile on her lips. She nodded, making the sign for *congratulations*. Her eyes lingered a bit on the two silent Englee people before she turned to leave.

I reached over and touched the box, surprised to find it made from nothing more than heavy kelp board. There was no lock or latch to hold the lid on. I tipped it off and peered inside. The box was filled with small leather-bound books. Real leather. The air was suddenly filled with the scent of them. Tanning chemicals and ink and the vanilla smell of aged paper rose from the box and surprised me. It was soothing in an odd way. And faintly familiar.

Aaka.

I pulled the box closer to me and grabbed a journal. But again I was stopped, this time by the gloved hand of one of the Englee people.

"First we must seal the agreement, Ms. Saakli."

"Nonsense," Uali growled from behind me. "She should be allowed to look at them first. These are hers regardless of the agreement."

The Englee paused, surprised by her reaction.

"We will need to prove the validity of the journals and make sure they are not tampered with. Agreed?"

We all nodded.

"Agreed," I said as my fingers tightened around the journal.

I opened it up. The leather was dark and slick from

repeated handling. I carefully thumbed through the thin pages, anxious to see what was inside. As soon as the writing came into focus, I recognized it. Tears blurred my vision, making the words dance. I had a few handmade birthday cards my mother had made me when I was a child, which now hung on my bedroom wall next to photos of her smiling face. She had never liked her own handwriting; she'd always thought it wasn't very feminine. But it represented her perfectly: simple, methodical, and measured.

I quickly read a few words. It seemed to be a recounting of sorts, detailing a trip she'd taken into the tundra, tracking wolves for three days. She mentioned finding exposed permafrost, noting the approximate depth, color, and size. Another page was about the different path a certain river took that year. For every place she mentioned, she wrote the GPS coordinates in the margins. I flipped to the middle of the book, to an entire page about fishing for grayling and accidentally snagging a whitefish. She recalled a story about her great-grandmother having done the same thing and how she had passed down that story as kind of a lesson: sometimes you get a different fish than you are trying for. On other pages, she wrote in detail about the activity of caribou in one part of the mountains, even taking time to describe the arrangement of their tracks, with direction coordinates and everything, noting how on the well-walked trails, their hooves dug deep into the earth, so deep that they released buried nutrients that looked like an oil slick on the surface of the mud. She listed the types of plants that grew along the old tracks and the newer ones. She talked about harvesting them and planning the harvest for the next year. In between the sentences, you could feel her love for the Arctic wild and all its nuances and whims. These journals were a treasure trove not only of scientific knowledge but also of cultural knowledge. It was obvious why she had placed them in the care of the Center.

My vision cleared as two tears made hot trails down my face. I could feel her reaching toward me from the past. I could almost smell the loam in her hair. I quickly set down the journal, blinking rapidly to dry my eyes before they could be seen by the Englee. Elder Uali and my aunt turned their faces from me, giving me a moment to collect myself. These emotions were for later, when I could sit with Aunt Beck and Nuvu and talk about them in detail and turn them over and over like river stones so they are smooth.

The smaller of the government representatives stepped forward, and with a little bit of a shiver, they removed their head cowl and sunglasses. The face underneath pinked immediately in the chilly air. It was a dark-haired woman around the same age as my aunt. Her heavy brows were drawn down in a V-shaped scowl.

"We will take the journals with us now to see if there is usable information. They will be returned to you as soon as the information is transferred to our teams." She opened her jacket and pulled out a synth tablet of her own. "All you have to do is place your hand on the tab, and the agreement will be sealed."

I stared at the screen in front of me. I made the hand gesture for *one minute*, and she frowned. My stomach roiled, and my hand tightened around the edge of the box.

"This is the agreement we made," she said, turning her attention to Elder Uali.

"She asked for a moment to collect herself, *Government*." Elder Uali moved to stand next to me. Her small frame was suddenly very comforting.

"We don't have a ton of time, Elder. We were told to retrieve the journals and fly back on the next flight to Newport Way."

Elder Uali waved her hand at the taller woman in dismissal and mimicked her frown.

I could feel the tension rising in the air like the metallic smell before a big storm. My ears popped as I felt my blood pressure go up. I quickly placed the top back on the box, hiding the scent of leather and vanilla. I saw the hard lines of Elder Uali's face, the stiffness in her fists, and I decided then and there.

I took a deep breath and cleared my suddenly dry throat to get everyone's attention.

"I will not be turning them over." My hands went up as all eyes suddenly turned in my direction. "I suspect there is much more to these journals, and I . . . I just can't." The short Englee woman stepped forward and took a breath. I spoke the next words before she had a chance to say something. "But I will go through them and give you the coordinates you want."

"You can't possibly read them as fast as our scanners. It's inefficient. We need the coordinates quickly. Our teams are combing through hundreds of locations; it takes thousands of man-hours to find and extract the samples we need. We have a deadline, and it might take you weeks to find what we're looking for in these books. We need to take them now."

No. Not now, not ever.

What are my options?

"Days." I said quickly, "Give me a handful of days, and I will get you what you want. A week at most. What do you have to lose? If I fail or if the coordinates prove false, we will not benefit either."

Her eyes glinted like fractured obsidian. She glanced once at her partner and then stepped around the corner as she tapped away at her tablet. I assumed she was consulting with someone higher up. I clasped my hands together to try to stop the tremble in them. I took a deep breath and turned to my aunt and Elder Uali, afraid to read their reactions. I expected them to be angry but was instead met with a mix of worry and sympathy.

At least I have that.

We could hear low, angry murmuring coming from around the corner. When the Englee woman returned, her face was a bit less pink. "You are given three days, and that is it. If fruitful coordinates are not provided, then our deal with the Elders is null. We wish you the best, Allu Saakli. We will be in contact." With that, she turned and beckoned to her partner, donned her cowl and glasses, and walked away.

The silence was heavy. I shifted from one foot to the other. I rubbed my palms together to try to dry the sweat on them. Taking a deep breath, I squared my shoulders, an attempt to look more confident than I felt, and turned back to face Uali and Aunt Beck. They looked nervous.

Allu, you got this. Whatever this *is. You got it.*

———

The next three days, I felt like a ghost. Translucent and barely there. The days and nights blurred into a haze of coffee and aching shoulder muscles as we sat hunched over the books, surrounded by silence.

Uali, Aunt Beck, Nuvu, his sister Carla, and I sat around the dining room table, carefully working through every single page. We synced our tablets so we could cross-check any information we found and weed out duplicates. We copied passages into the master file we would turn over with the coordinates for reference. There were about a hundred small journals packed into the box, arranged by date, with the oldest at the top and the newest at the bottom. We resisted talking about what we found in them, afraid that even that little bit of time would be a waste.

We were about halfway through the books before I found myself. My mother had noted that there was a link between the number of berries that year and the larger-than-normal fields of tundra cotton. Then she had written that the berries were larger than normal and mentioned how much I would enjoy picking them, as they would be easier for my chubby fingers to grab. She talked about how much I loved cloudberries with a splash of heavy cream in a bowl.

I stopped reading for a minute and let the emotions rise in my chest.

Abruptly, I wasn't a ghost—I existed. I was about six years old when she went missing, still a child, still not aware of anything other than her being Aaka. I never even got to see her as Hera. I never got to hear these stories at her side in her own words. As I inhaled the sweet smell of the books, my chest stuttered with grief again. Grief I'd thought had long since been smoothed over.

What would you think of me now, Aaka? Did I make the right decision?

The scraping of a chair on the floor made me look up. Nuvu was scooting his chair closer to mine so that his shoulder touched my back. He quickly made another shared file, and we all began dumping paragraphs in whenever we found a reference or story about me.

I was more than tempted to find a nook and dive into the file.

Later, I told myself as I gritted my teeth, wiped my face, and dove back into the pile of books.

On the third day, I took a few hours to go through all of the information we had gathered. The amount was staggering. I realized that my mother must have kept these journals since she was about my age, when she'd found her passion and her means of service to her people.

At one point, Elder Uali pulled me aside. She had found a passage that was a bit complicated. It was about the remains of ancient wooly mammoths, frozen deep in a crevasse near the edge of the mountains where they met the sea. The remains were somewhat hard to access; Hera had been exploring a mile-long fissure in the earth using mountain-climbing gear when she found them. The issue was that the coordinates were at the edge of the calving grounds for the largest of our caribou herds—normally forbidden territory for outsiders. Uali worried that if they timed their search wrong, they could disturb the caribou migration to such an extent that it could take years to return to normal. The caribou herd was essential to our food stores for the winter, so any change could have dire consequences. We carefully laid out a plan for when and how the government should approach the area, giving them a window in which to retrieve the remains that would hopefully avoid disturbing the herd.

To outsiders, the information and timing and locations might have seemed like just interesting stories and colorful anecdotes, but to our people, these small bits and pieces were more. They were the cogs and gears of our identity, a worldview and existence that was wholly unique.

And that was worth protecting, no matter what Raven promised.

A couple months later, I found myself slipping my new ceremonial parka over my head. It was heavier than I thought it would be. I bent over and pulled the hem into view. The six-inch-wide decoration at the bottom was a masterpiece of carefully sewn tiny pieces of leather and fur depicting tuttu walking on the tundra. Caribou were travelers like my mother, and maybe someday soon, I would be a traveler, too. Except for me, it would be traveling the sea of stars to unknown places light-years away. I smiled and ran my hand over the intricate trim. Elder Uali had made it herself, knowing my aunt was not the sewing type. The weight of the skins and leather felt solid on my shoulders. *I* felt solid.

Later, I stood at the end of the hall, a small crowd gathered around Elder Uali and my aunt and me. The celebrations had been going all day, and now it was time for the grand finale: the Naming. It became quiet suddenly as everyone felt the shift in the crowd.

Elder Uali stood in front of me and placed her tiny bird-like hands on my cheeks. I had to bend down a little, which made the hood of my parka shelter us both like an umbrella, the sounds of the people in the room muffled. She smiled at me, glints of merriment in her eyes. She smelled like the years that were between us.

"Allu Saakli," she said, "daughter of our People, daughter of our lands—we, the Elders of the Real People, give you a name. We give you the name Hera. For your mother to be reborn in you. For her to be reborn in this world."

My whole life, I had felt adrift, like a fireseed in the wind, never knowing where I would land. Seeds do not get to choose where they end up being planted.

TWIN STRANGERS

ELIZABETH BEAR

I was sitting on the bed, tweaking my digital twin, when Jaxx showed up for class. He was early. He came up the ladder to my loft over the cab, leaned over my shoulder before I knew he was there, and said, "Nobody really looks like that, Liam."

I dropped my screen facedown so fast I nearly fumbled it onto the floor. I whipped my headphones off.

"Crap!" I yelled. "I nearly pissed myself!"

"Liam! Language!" Mom Stacy yelled from the back of the RV.

"Sorry, Mom."

"Noise-canceling," Jaxx said, ignoring the existence of parents and picking up the headphones. "Great until you don't want to get snuck up on. You might have seen me in that mirror"—he pointed to the one on the bulkhead, crammed into the corner—"if you hadn't thrown a shirt over it. What are you doing?"

"Clothes shopping." I tried to sound bored.

He flopped down on the bed beside me. "Anyway, you

shouldn't mess with your dop's measurements. You can lie to your parents. You can lie to your shrink. You can lie to your priest—"

"I haven't got a priest."

"—but don't lie to your dop. The results always suck."

I snorted. My dop's image was derived from footage my device had captured of me over the years. I didn't see anything weirder about adjusting its measurements than adjusting its gender. "I'm not trying to fool anybody."

That was also a lie.

"Your clothes aren't gonna fit," he said idly.

"I'll just have to fit the clothes."

"If you keep corrupting its data, it'll probably enter you in a bodybuilding contest. And then you'll have to do it, or all the girls you like will know you're chicken."

"I don't like any girls." Another lie. I took my headphones away from him. "Go get yours—it's time for class."

We had ten more minutes, but I didn't want to talk about it anymore.

Jaxx comes over to my place for class because his family is #vanlife on a small scale and there's no quiet or privacy over there. With two kid brothers, not even a headset would help. My place is closer to the Wi-Fi node, we've got a booster, and I have my own little room up over the cab. We can sit on my bed and do school on our remote days.

My moms even got Jaxx a set of noise-canceling head-phones to use at our place and told him they were spares. That way, they stay with us and nothing happens to them, like it would if he took them home. Jaxx isn't absentminded, so I know it's not him who breaks or loses everything.

Halfway through history, I glanced over at Jaxx and noticed he was grinning down at his screen. The Magna Carta just wasn't that interesting. He was still in class—at least, I saw him down in the corner on my screen, looking like he was paying attention.

I leaned over to peek at his screen. He was playing Zaladoz, which, okay, is a supercool tower defense game but *definitely* not schoolwork.

He jerked his screen away from me, but I'd already seen. I muted my headset. "Mx. Seaman is gonna be pissed if they realize you've got your dop sitting in class for you."

"Shh!"

I showed him the mute light.

"Look, there's no reason at all for this class to be synchronous! It's crap that we have to be here in real time when we could, I dunno, listen to this boring-ass lecture while we sleep."

"Dude."

"Sleep learning is a real thing!"

I pointed to Jaxx's dop on my screen. "And isn't that supposed to be blocked?"

He tried to look modest. "I jailbroke it. Crap, they're calling on me." He unmuted hastily—"King John!"—and muted again.

I mouthed, *You're gonna get in so much trouble*, but Jaxx was already back to building towers and staffing them with flying monkeys.

After class, we slithered down the ladder. Mom Stacy was at work, tucked into the booth behind the table with her headset on. She looked up and waved as we came into the kitchen. She'd already put protein powder, yogurt, baby spinach, and frozen bananas on the counter for smoothies. I made Jaxx's first, standing between her and the blender so she couldn't see that both bananas and most of the yogurt went into that one. He needed it more than I did, but she gets mad at me when I don't eat, even though I keep telling her I can't have carbs, like, at all except right after practice.

We went outside to drink the smoothies and sat on the fold-down steps. Jaxx must have been worrying the whole time, because as soon as the door was shut, he looked at me and said, "You can't tell anyone."

"I just don't want you to get busted." It seemed like a good time to change the subject. My smoothie tasted like watery fake strawberry. "What about Kiara?"

"Oh no." He gestured so dramatically he got smoothie on his pants. "Don't you dare tell anybody about that, either."

Jaxx has a crush on Kiara. Jaxx should just *tell* Kiara he has a crush on her, but he's always got reasons not to. "Come on," I said, as I had six million and three times before. "What's the worst that could happen?"

He looked at me bleakly. "I could die of embarrassment."

"That's not real."

I was out of smoothie. I took his empty glass and carried both of them inside to put in the sink.

"It's totally real!" he called after me. "You get so embarrassed you just melt. *Glub*."

We parked our dops and left them behind. Jaxx stuck his in the school social space, running in bot mode so he could come back to the conversations later and see if anyone had said anything interesting. If someone needed his attention right away, they could text or use the override code. My dop was still trying on jeans, and I figured he couldn't get into too much trouble, so I left the program running.

I always felt weird turning him off, anyway. It was like turning off a friend.

I started jogging slowly, warming up. Jaxx raced to catch up and then pressed his hands to his belly theatrically. "I am so full of smoothie I can feel it slosh."

"No puking," I said. I still felt kind of weird and awkward because he'd seen me reprogramming my dop. Despite what he said, there's nothing wrong with wanting to reflect your true self with an avatar that fits your self-image, is there? Mx. Seaman does.

Jaxx and I ran over to the field house for wrestling practice. It's about three miles, and we can do it in about twenty minutes. It was hot and humid—it's always hot and humid; we haven't had a real freeze here in New Jersey since I was ten—so the run helped us sweat down a couple of pounds. Since I'm always trying to cut weight, that works out.

Jaxx is wiry and he's got a light frame. It doesn't matter for him. But for me, every ounce counts.

We ran through the park, between vans and RVs, then onto

the dirt trail under the trees. It runs alongside the highway, but there's a chain-link fence and a load of dirt bike jumps made out of plywood. Nobody uses it but kids. We've traveled all up and down the East Coast and as far west as Rapid City, though we've been here since I was in fifth grade because Moms care about my "social development" and don't want to take me away from all my friends. There's always places like this. Sometimes you find a grown-up back there, a trail biker or a dog walker, but mostly it's like they've forgotten those trails even exist. I guess once you're driving, you don't need 'em anymore.

"Wouldn't it be cool if dops were real?" I wanted to pant, but I made myself talk in a normal-ish tone.

"They are real," Jaxx said. *He* didn't sound out of breath at all.

"They're not *real* real." He sped up, and I had to push. The heat made me light-headed. "They're not *people*."

"What, like an AI?"

"Sure." Now I *was* gasping.

"No good—they'd just destroy humanity. Take over, rule the earth. Like Terminators."

I don't know why everybody assumes that a superior intelligence is just going to want to wipe out humankind. On the other hand, maybe there's something about our self-image that explains why we assume that's what a superior intelligence would decide.

"Dinosaur," I told Jaxx.

"You're a dinosaur," he answered. "You're not *even* a dinosaur, because dinosaurs are cool. And even my mom uses a dop, so dops are for dinosaurs, too."

I didn't have breath to argue because we were racing now, giggling, shoving, bursting out in between trees and onto the grass behind the field house. We pelted across the lawn, feet thudding, and slammed into the corrugated wall. He got there half a second before I did. I gave him an extra shove for good measure.

We pushed each other through the door and into the locker room. Coach Jode frowned at us over his screen when we came in, and we quieted down, sort of. Still giggling.

"Strip down," he told us. "On the scale."

The *worst.* I did it, and I was only three pounds over. The match wasn't until the weekend. I had time; I could cut another pound and a half by then and make up the difference in the steam box. And then, I told myself, I was going to eat the biggest hot fudge sundae the world had ever seen.

I stared at myself in the mirror while Jaxx weighed in, looking at my eyes because it was too upsetting to look at my body. I blurred my vision and imagined my dop there instead. I could picture him looking tight, six-pack and a cut groin. He grinned at me in my imagination and waved jauntily. I waved back.

"Come on, Snickerbach," said Coach, tapping me on the shoulder. "Quit admiring your reflection and get your shorts on. All right, everybody! Hit the mats."

My reflection turned purple. I whirled away from him, living proof that you *can't* die from embarrassment after all. I didn't manage to get my shorts and shoes on without tripping, but at least I just hopped around like an idiot instead of falling over and bashing my teeth out on a bench.

I got my ass kicked six times at practice and could not have been happier that Friday was weight training. Coach stopped me on the way to the showers. "What's going on?"

"Skipped lunch," I said.

He gave me The Look. "You need to eat, kid."

"I got busy!"

He waved me on, but I don't think he believed me.

I wandered home, ate the salmon and salad Mom Elisa had made, and pushed the brown rice around on my plate. After dinner, I went upstairs, looked through the jeans my dop had picked out, and decided I only liked one pair, so I sent those to Moms for approval.

If I didn't get my weight down *and* start performing better in practice, I was going to get cut from the team. Jaxx was lighter and better than me, though I was stronger. I needed to get myself together, or he was going to beat me out. I texted about it with my dop for an hour or so, but it didn't make me any less worried. He's a good listener, having no real life of his own. But he's not great at solutions.

Thursday was pretty much the same, though I only got beat three times. Jaxx and I were out of the showers, toweled off, dressed, and lacing up our shoes when Coach came in, looking unhappy. "Cruz."

Nobody likes to hear that tone in a teacher's voice. Jaxx jumped guiltily, then got to his feet. "Coach?"

"You're wanted in the principal's office. In person! Well, go on."

I slouched home alone. At least it was cooler out now. Moms had finished dinner by the time I got home, and Mom Stacy was washing up. "There's a plate in the fridge," she said. "Help yourself."

"Okay, but I grabbed a sandwich with Jaxx after practice. I'm not super hungry."

"Wow, when I was your age, I could eat a whole pizza. *And* dessert. And by then, I'd have room for another pizza." She put the last plate in the drying rack. "I'm out of the kitchen!"

Mom Elisa came out of the bathroom, drying her hair. "I just remembered it was my turn to cook."

"You came home absolutely fried," Mom Stacy said. "You can't take care of anybody else unless you also take care of yourself, and you can't take care of yourself unless you're kind to yourself."

"Fine," Mom Elisa answered, pretending to scold. "But I'm doing the next two nights."

Married twenty years and still disgusting. Life goals.

Oh man, Mom Stacy had made garlic bread. Pure torture. I tried not to smell the butter and olive oil and garlic while I filled up my plate with salad and two pieces of chicken Parmesan. While the chicken was heating up, I stirred the spaghetti around in the container to make it look like I'd taken some. I figured between the run and practice, the bread crumbs on the chicken would be okay.

I made myself eat slowly, though my stomach felt like an angry animal. When I'd just about licked the plate, I washed it off and put it in the rack beside the other two. Moms were in the living room part of the RV, cuddling on the couch and streaming some doctor show. Mom Elisa, who is Dr. Elisa Lopez, MD (I've got Mom Stacy's last name), is a float doc, and she likes to critique the medicine.

I don't even spend all day around sick people, and I can't stand hospital shows. Grown-ups are weird.

"I can scooch over," Mom Stacy said, but I waved my hand and said, "I'm going for a walk."

When I got to Jaxx's place, though, there didn't seem to be anybody home. Unless the weather's bad, their slot usually has people spilling out the sliding door and hanging out under the awning on the yard couch or at the picnic table until well past dark. The sun was still a finger above the trees, but the ugly brown van was locked up tight, a sunshade propped across the windshield.

All the bikes were gone, though. Maybe they were out for a ride.

I wandered around a bit more before texting Jaxx.

hey man. lil worried about you gettin pulled in
u ok

He didn't answer. I went home and got started on my assignments for class, but it was hard to concentrate. Jaxx always texted me back, like, right away. I hoped he hadn't gotten his phone privileges revoked.

I tried getting my dop to talk to his, but his was offline and set to no messages.

In bed, while I was lying there listening to my stomach growl and thinking about burning calories, I tried one more time. hey what's up. u ok?

Nothing answered me but the sound of the cicadas droning through the louvers on the windows.

I woke up the next morning, rolled over, and grabbed my phone, and the first thing I found was a message from that girl Jaxx liked, Kiara. What the hell is wrong with you?!

I replied, what are you talking about???

No answer.

Just as well I didn't have any appetite for breakfast, I guess. I grabbed a cup of coffee—"It'll stunt your growth!" (Mom Stacy)—and slithered back up the ladder in time for class. I'd shower after lifting and save on water. I had plenty of time to comb my hair. After that, I had nothing to do but bust out a hundred push-ups, then hang out on my phone and wait for Jaxx.

Five minutes before class, Mom Stacy yelled up the ladder, "Isn't Jaxx coming today?"

I looked at the unanswered texts on my phone. There was a horrible sensation inside me, like when you fall out of a bunk bed in the middle of the night.

"He didn't say anything. Maybe he's sick?" I almost told her that he'd gotten into some kind of trouble at school, but it would have embarrassed him, so I kept my mouth shut.

"Well, if he's late, there's some extra cereal in the cupboard."

Oh man, if Jaxx didn't turn up, I was going to have to figure out which one of the neighbors had a dog that liked smoothies.

I logged in.

First class on Thursdays was physics, which I liked a lot more than history. Jaxx was there, and so was Kiara. I tried to catch both their eyes and they both avoided me. So that was the real Jaxx, not Jaxx's dop. Also, every time he answered a question, I could hear his brothers screaming in the background. Confirmed.

I texted him again.

I might as well have been texting Santa Claus.

After class, lunch was leftovers. I had salad again and left a plate with a piece of chicken up in my loft for after practice. Ran over to the field house and hit the weights without bothering to change. I was just going to run home again in the same clothes. It didn't matter if they got *more* sweaty.

Jaxx didn't show.

My form sucked. I couldn't concentrate, and I kept checking my phone to see if I'd missed a text. My whole body ached with some emotion I didn't really have a name for. Maybe it was anxiety.

It felt gross.

I had just finished a miserable set of hamstring curls and rolled over when I realized Coach was standing right over me. I blinked up at him. I probably looked like a goldfish when its tank pump stops working.

"Good to see you," he said.

I should have kept my mouth shut and played it cool, but some people have those genes and I . . . just don't. "Why wouldn't I be here?"

Coach scrubbed his hand across his mouth. "Sometimes guys drop out after their friends get cut."

"Oh," I said, head spinning. I managed not to say anything dumb. I just nodded.

He slapped me on the shoulder and walked away. I stared after him. I couldn't focus my eyes. That little animal burrowing in my gut felt like the time I ate way too many green peaches. I slung myself off the bench and jogged to the men's room.

Jaxx got cut from the team?

Jaxx got *cut*?

He was twice as good a wrestler as I was, and he never had a problem making weight. Why would he get cut before me?

I couldn't lift so good after that, but I faked it for a half hour, then ran back to the park like six mean dogs were after me.

I was sure—I was *sure*—that by the time I got to the park Jaxx's van would be gone and there would be nothing where it had been parked except an empty lot with grass growing in it, or maybe a completely different RV. But the ugly brown van was there, and the kids and toys and rugs and plastic tables spilling out onto the dusty ground.

Jaxx was out there with both his brothers, lying on a rug on his stomach, watching them play with blocks. I stopped at the edge of the rug, and he looked up, made a face, and pushed up onto his knees. "Shove off."

I stared at him. Then I sat down in the dirt cross-legged and said, "You don't have to take it out on me."

"Who else should I take it out on? It's your fault."

How could it be my fault? I didn't even know what was going on. "Wait, what? Jaxx, let's go for a walk."

He pointed at the kids with his chin. "Babysitting. And I don't want to talk to you."

"Do you want me to quit the team? Because I will, if you're jealous—"

He whispered, I imagine so his brothers wouldn't hear. "Jealous! You're the one who's jealous. I mean, I assume that's why you did it."

"Did *what*?"

You know how some people can stare at you as if you're a complete jerk and stupid to boot? He had the knack. "Turned me in."

That feeling like I was falling out of an airplane was just getting worse. "I did *not*."

Jaime had started hitting José over the head, but he was using his fist instead of the blocks and José was a lot bigger, so I decided to let either them or Jaxx sort it out. I shoved my hands into my pockets.

Jaxx might not have noticed the kids. He snorted. "You were the only one who knew I was cutting class. Anyway, Kiara told me you told her I liked her when she let me down easy yesterday afternoon. So thanks for *that*, also."

I pulled my hands out of my pockets, but then they were

just kind of swinging in the breeze, so I crossed my arms over my chest instead. "I did no such thing."

"Oh, so now she's a liar, too?"

"Come on, Jaxx. You know I'm not like that. You could have come to me and asked!"

He simpered mockingly. "There's two sides to every story."

"Yes, and one of those sides is a lie." I wanted to hit something. I jumped up and started pacing back and forth. Now *I* was mad at *him*. "You didn't come to me when you heard that. You didn't ask. You just made up a story in your head and blamed me. We've been friends since fifth grade! When you busted yourself up on your bike and were stuck in the hammock all summer, I came over every single day and played games with you. I missed out on everything else!"

"Yeah, well . . . somebody ratted me out." He made finger guns and shot me with them, *bang-bang.*

I tried to walk in looking normal, but apparently I wasn't very good at it because Mom Elisa stopped in the middle of making chicken and broccoli and frowned at me. She traveled a lot for work, and it was nice to have her home. But she was too damn perceptive.

She said, "Something's wrong."

Without really meaning to, I found myself telling her, "Jaxx got cut from the wrestling team for cheating on his classes, and he thinks I turned him in."

"Did you?"

I shook my head.

"You know," she said, paying very close attention to the chicken she was slicing, "if you knew he was cheating and didn't say anything, you could get in trouble, too."

"Thanks, Mom," I said. "That was just the emotional support I needed."

"Liam."

I sighed. "I know, I know. You're just looking out for me. Well, I've got a ton of homework."

"It must feel pretty bad," she said.

The moment had passed, though. I headed toward the ladder. "Yell when dinner is ready."

I beat it up to my room and pulled the shutter closed. I did not want to eat that chicken. I wrapped it up in a worn-out sock and stuffed it in the wastebasket. I'd take it out before dinner.

I *did* open my homework, but I found myself staring at it without any ability to concentrate. So I put my headset on and called up my dop.

Just looking at him was soothing. He was lean and shark-like, still wearing the jeans I'd picked out. They looked good on him.

He didn't look anything like me, did he? I reached out across the narrow space and pulled the shirt off my mirror. I needed a shave, which was exciting. Nope, I was definitely kidding myself about those biceps. Among another things.

As I looked from my own reflection to the dop, that free-fall feeling inside me clotted into actual horror. I tapped the screen to open the settings menu and asked, "Activity report since Wednesday morning?"

"Hi, Liam," my dop said. Since it was reporting to me, it sounded more mechanical than when we were just having a conversation. "Regular system maintenance, user edit, clothes shopping (see inline document for 572 jeans options), report clothing choices to Moms, report to school—"

"Wait," I said.

The dop froze.

"Details on that last one."

"Sure," said the dop. "As your agent, I contacted the anonymous report line at Judy Blume Senior High School to inform them of what you discussed with me last night concerning Jaxx Cruz—"

"Stop." I closed my eyes. "I'm not a—" I realized Moms were still downstairs and lowered my voice. "I'm not a snitch!"

"Social models indicate with eighty-three percent confidence that you would have wanted me to take care of that for you. As your virtual assistant, I—"

"Stop."

He did. He was just software, after all. Just following orders.

"Stop using the technical language. Just talk to me."

"Sure, Liam."

"Why would you do that?" I asked.

"Because we're jealous of Jaxx," he said. "And now we don't have to feel so bad. And because you told him not to cheat, and he blew you off, and that made you feel bad, too."

I almost dropped the screen.

Jaxx had been right. I'd lied to my dop, and in so doing, I'd made it not my twin at all. I'd trained the algorithm to behave in ways I hadn't anticipated, somehow. So its best guess of what I had wanted my dop to do when I'd talked my problems out to it hadn't been very good at all.

I guess it's true, what Mom Stacy says—if you don't like yourself, if you're not kind to yourself, you can't be a good friend to anyone else, either. And it turns out that if you don't like yourself, you can train your dop to be a bad friend, too.

Maybe Jaxx had been right to blame me. I felt terrible. But I also felt angry. So angry I wanted to go outside and run around in the woods and kick trees. Except I'd have to get past Moms to do that, and I didn't want to talk about it.

Also, it was dark outside, so there would be a fight about me leaving. And possibly bears.

I buried my face in my pillow and didn't scream loud enough to bother Moms.

I hoped.

Well, there was something I could do about wanting to scream and run around in the dark hitting things. I grabbed my screen and pulled the blanket up to hide the glow. Those noise-canceling headphones are also great for when I want to play games in the middle of the night without Moms catching on. I took my virtual self into Etern X and chased werewolves through a beautifully rendered forest. Every so often, I caught one and threw it into a tree trunk.

Cheaper than therapy.

I was right to feel betrayed and terrible, I decided. But maybe I was also right to be a little bit mad at Jaxx. He could have tried harder to find out what had happened instead of just blaming me.

I looked at myself in the mirror again. Then I looked at my dop, comically muscular and lean, paused with a werewolf in his fist. No, he wasn't me. He wasn't what I wanted to be, either.

I logged out of Etern X, then scrolled down in the settings and found the toggle to reset the defaults to scanned-in information only. My finger hovered for fifteen seconds.

Then I hit it, and before I could think about it too much, I pressed confirm.

I slid down the ladder into the kitchen the next morning to a chorus of Moms yelling, "Three points of contact!"

Sigh.

It's not like I'm going to pull the ladder off the wall. It's bolted there.

I felt so sorry for myself that I grabbed one of Mom Elisa's diet sodas instead of coffee, even though those things make you bloat. Seriously, she's a medical professional. You'd think she'd take better care of herself.

Then I realized both Moms were sitting at the kitchen table, even though Mom Elisa usually leaves for work long before I get out of bed. She gets Sundays off and an alternating Tuesday or Thursday. It was Saturday, so she should have been long out the door.

I pulled my head out of the fridge and said, "What's wrong?"

"Nothing's *wrong*," Mom Stacy said. "Come sit down."

"I have a study date in five minutes." If I could just escape back up the ladder, I could avoid the bad news, whatever it was. I edged a step away.

"This will only take a few minutes," said Mom Elisa.

I sat on the very edge of the built-in bench with, like, half my butt so I could make a quick getaway when they were done.

"I have a job offer in San Francisco," Mom Elisa said. "But it's a five-year contract. Good pay, and the Bay Area is amazing. I think you'd love it—"

"You promised I could finish school here!" I yelped. "And I just made varsity—" I was going to unmake it again in a hurry if I didn't get my act together, but never undermine your own argument. I learned that one from Mom Elisa herself.

"I know," she said. "Don't interrupt. I'm not finished."

"Sorry." I opened the soda for something to do with my hands.

She turned her tea mug between hers. "We're not going to make you switch schools unless you want to. Stacy and I can do a long-distance thing for a while, and she can stay here with you. Her job doesn't care where she is. I do, but we can make it work until you leave for college. Or, if you want, we can all go out together and you can telecommute to school. The Bay Area has a youth wrestling club that's supposed to be excellent, and some of the schools have an athlete exchange program now. And there are beaches and mountains. You get a driver's license this year."

I almost said, "I'd have to leave Jaxx," but I remembered in time and took a drink of soda instead. It hurt my teeth and burned my throat. Well, I guess the stuff *is* acid.

Mom Stacy reached out and grabbed my hand. "Think about it," she said. "You don't have to decide right now."

"What if I want you to stay here?" I said to Mom Elisa.

She pursed her lips and nodded, then looked at Mom Stacy.

Mom Stacy nodded, too.

"I would," said Mom Elisa. "But the pay out there is a lot better. You wouldn't have to apply for scholarships *and* take out student loans. Or stick to in-state schools and commute."

"Crap," I said. "How long do I have to think about this?"

"I'm leaving in two weeks if I take the job," Mom Elisa said. "I can give you until Monday night to decide what you want."

I did have a study date, but, surprising nobody, neither Jaxx nor Kiara showed up for it. I needed to talk to Jaxx so bad it was like an itch inside me. I probably also needed to talk to Kiara; I was pretty sure she was mad at me because my dop had texted her and ratted out Jaxx to her, too. And probably told her about his crush.

I hadn't asked, because I didn't really want to know beyond a shadow of a doubt.

But I sort of knew anyway.

I lay there on the bed pretending I understood quadratic equations and intermittently texting Jaxx, begging him to call me, until it dawned on me that he probably had my number blocked.

I didn't want to leave. I did want to leave. I could just duck away from this mistake and start over, and it wouldn't cost me anything except a spot on the team. I could get away from Kiara and Jaxx. Make some friends who would never find out about how dumb I'd been.

And, you know . . . California. I wondered if the Bay Area had surfing or if that was just southern California. I wondered if it had surfer girls.

I could message Jaxx through the school system, but I didn't think either one of us wanted there to be an official record of this conversation. I could text, dop, or call Kiara and beg her to beg Jaxx to call me. If she hadn't blocked me, too.

I was too scared to find out. Though at least she'd had the guts to cuss me out to my face.

It took me forty-five minutes to realize that maybe Jaxx hadn't blocked my dop from contacting his. And another forty-five minutes to write the message, because I didn't trust my dop to pick the language anymore.

And then it took me an hour to work up the nerve to send it.

Hey, I need to talk. Moms want to move me to the West Coast. I figured out who ratted on you.

Please, Jaxx.

By then, it was basically time for lunch. I went downstairs and messed around with protein powder and a pear and some yogurt. It actually tasted okay and it didn't make my stomach do any more backflips than it was already.

I was drinking the last of my smoothie when my phone dinged, which caused an additional backflip. Feelings are the worst.

It was my dop, relaying a message from Jaxx. **Meet me by the trail.**

"Mom," I called—not too loud, because Mom Stacy was ten feet away on the couch. "I'm going for a run."

Jaxx was there. I had kinda thought he wouldn't be. He wouldn't meet my eyes, and he was kicking rocks, but he was there.

"All right, what do you want?" he mumbled.

"My moms want to move to California."

"Easy out," he said.

"Look," I said. "They're willing to do a long-distance thing until I graduate. But I can't decide what to do until I find out what you want."

He stared at me. The dark circles under his eyes made them seem sad and huge. "You said you knew who ratted me out."

"My dop," I said. "I messed with its programming too much, and it . . . kinda went rogue, I guess."

Jaxx stared at me harder, one eyebrow creeping up. He practices that in the mirror, but that doesn't make me feel any less like an idiot when he does it. "I told you."

"Yeah," I said. "I know."

He sighed and knuckled his eyes. "Well, I'm still mad."

"Look," I said, "I understand that you're hurt and upset. I made a mistake, but I didn't mean to, and you made a mistake, too. It was a dick move not to trust me enough to ask me what happened before you ditched me. And I'm still pretty pissed off, too." I took a big breath. "You can still come over and do class at my place. And if you want to, I'll ask to stay. We don't have to be friends, but . . . man, your place is a *zoo*."

He made a face. "Let me think about it. Give me a couple of days."

Jaxx didn't show up on Monday, but I did get a text. Still thinking.

So I guess he had unblocked me. After school, I skipped lunch and went over to the field house early. I ran my butt off, put in an extra lap around the soccer field, and still managed to get stuck camping out on the steps and waiting for somebody to come unlock the building.

I sat there in the sun, hanging out on my phone and trying not to feel horrible about myself every time I looked at my dop. Maybe if I just kind of . . . didn't think about it too much, I'd start to not mind. I dunno, maybe it was working? Anyway, I was feeling sort of halfway decent for the first time in days when Coach Jode walked up along the wall behind me. "You want to tell me anything, Snickerbach?"

I jumped so hard I skinned my ankle on the step.

He didn't laugh. Coach isn't such a bad guy.

I looked at him looking at me and said, "I hate my last name. What the hell were they thinking at Ellis Island?"

That time, he did laugh. After a decent pause, he said, "I noticed you haven't been doing so well since Cruz got cut."

"He blames me," I said. "And he's got a right to, I guess. But I'm pretty mad at him, too, because he's been my best friend for, like, a million years, and he still assumed I was a bad guy without talking to me about it first."

Out of the corner of my eye, I saw Coach nodding slowly. "Huh. That's rough. But give it some time, see what happens."

I braced for him to tell me I was young and none of this would seem so important in a year. Instead, he pointed to the cement steps. "Can we chat?"

I nodded, and he flopped down beside me. The light caught his face funny, and he almost looked like a real person for a minute, not a teacher. He didn't look at me, just stared off across the lawn toward the trees, his lips pressed together and his jaw tight.

"Am I getting cut, too?" I asked when I couldn't stand it anymore. That would solve my moving dilemma, anyway. If there was no Jaxx and I wasn't on the team, well . . .

He looked at me, and his eyebrows went up. "Sorry," he said. "I guess I was drawing out the suspense a little. No, nothing like that. But I think you ought to go up a weight class."

"But I can make weight, Coach. I can do this!"

"I know you can." He sighed. "But there's a difference between being *able* to do something and it being a good idea. And it's going to keep getting harder. You're already starting to fill out."

"Coach—"

"C'mon, Snickerbach. You get your butt handed to you because you're hungry all the time. That's not wrestling up to your potential."

I looked at my hands. They were veiny and gaunt. "All

right." Then I had to change the subject. "How'd you wind up a wrestling coach?"

"I could have made better choices." He took a deep breath and sighed. "But I didn't."

"Your dad didn't pay enough attention to you?" I asked.

He frowned at me. I winced, sure I was about to get cut from the team after all. Then he shook his head and laughed with his mouth closed.

"I could have used a little more guidance," he admitted. "Now, get out there and give me ten laps!"

I got up. I felt . . . not good, but okay. Pretty okay. Jaxx was going to have to make his own choices.

But I had made mine. If Moms were actually okay with commuting cross-country to see each other for a while, I figured I could stand to stick around and try to fix things with my best friend.

And hey, maybe I—maybe Jaxx and I both—could go out to California to visit. *And* to find out about those surfers.

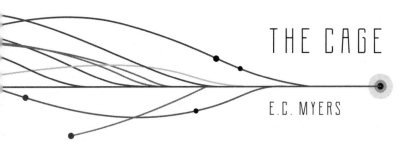

THE CAGE

E.C. MYERS

**Excerpt from SimonSez Channel on GLiTCH.tv,
livestreamed on May 18, 2034, 9:42 p.m. ET.
Transcript annotated with AI-generated
video description.**

Hello? Is this live?

*[Close-up on black-haired, pale teen. They
have dark shadows under their eyes, and their
white T-shirt is wrinkled. The teen leans
closer to the camera and then pulls back.]*

I think we're good. I hope this is getting
out. Even if no one's watching now, it'll be
online forever—internet immortality for the
win! Unless the Freedom School has this video
removed. If anyone *is* watching, you might want
to download a backup copy. Just in case.

Anyway. I'm Simon Shin. You might have heard of me from the *Inexplicable* podcast. Hi, Ogden. You always wanted to hear my side of the story. Well, here it is: the Cage.

[The teen turns the camera and focuses on a small, cube-shaped log cabin with a plain wooden door, locked with a thick padlock. A metal rod extends up from the flat roof and off-screen.]

As you can see, I'm here at the scene of the "crime." I mean, I'd call it more of an accident, maybe. A breakthrough, if I were being pretentious. Like I've been saying all along, the only crimes Nicky and I committed were violating curfew, misappropriating school resources, violating the school internet and technology terms of service . . . well, that's probably more than my lawyer would want me to admit on video.

[The camera zooms in on the padlock, which is broken. The teen turns the camera back to their face.]

Let's add breaking and entering, though we'll hold off on the entering part, because I don't want to lose my 7G signal. Oh, and I suppose we also broke some fundamental laws of physics, depending on how you look at it. But I don't know any government or court of law that would hold us accountable for that.

[Lightning flashes and thunder rumbles. The teen laughs.]

Wow, talk about perfect timing. Nicky would say I'm "trying to be theatrical," but they like that about me. Besides, theater is how we met in the first place.

[The teen looks back at the cabin for a moment.]

They're planning to tear this building down in a few days, so I'm running out of time. We're expecting another big storm tonight, just like the night they disappeared six months ago, so this is probably my last chance to get Nicky back, one way or another.

[The teen turns the camera back to the square cabin.]

It's been treated like some international mystery, but what happened that night is only important to Nicky, their parents, and me. Okay, and some scientists who are really going to have their minds blown when they see this.

But the real story is what's been happening at this school.

[The theme song to the Inexplicable *podcast plays.]*

And that's Ogden calling. Again. Obviously, I'm not going to answer that. Stay tuned.

« « » »

Inexplicable **Podcast, Episode 41:**
"Where Is Nicky?"
Published on the TrueCrime Podcast Network
on April 1, 2034
{transcript}

OGDEN LAKE: The morning of November 15, 2033, began like any other for Nicky Montana. Their smart clock records show that they switched off the alarm at 6:40 a.m. after hitting snooze once and listening to "Trouble with Dreams" on the radio for five minutes. Not surprising, since that song is listed as one of their favorites on their S0ci@1 profile.

Still in bed, Nicky unlocked their phone and spent the next ten minutes catching up on S0ci@1 posts, leaving sixteen hearts on their mutuals' photos and a dozen generic, encouraging comments. That was the kind of friend they were—they always had a kind word for everyone. These comments went into the school's queue for moderation and were posted eleven minutes later.

Nicky was up and showered by seven thirty, when they received a text message from Simon Shin: *Are you sure you want to do this?* Nicky responded five minutes later: *No, but we're going to do it anyway.*

From all accounts and evidence, Simon Shin was Nicky's closest friend. And he was the last person to see them alive . . . that same night.

Simon is likely the only person who has the answers we need about Nicky's mysterious disappearance, or at least the only person who knows the *questions* we should be asking. More on him in a moment.

But first, my name is Ogden Lake, and this is *Inexplicable*. Thank you for listening and subscribing. Each week, we look at a hot case that's cooling off: a crime, death, or disappearance that appears to have no solution. We work to discover the whereabouts of missing persons or the circumstances of their deaths by reconstructing their final hours and days. We get help from law enforcement, special investigators, concerned loved ones, and especially active listeners like you at home.

And boy, do we have an interesting one for you this time. This is our most intriguing mystery yet. Can *you* help solve it?

While you've probably heard the name Nicky Montana all over the news in recent months, you don't know the full story. Neither do we—*yet*. Like I said, only Simon Shin knows the truth, and he won't return my calls.

What makes this disappearance different from most? We know exactly when Nicky disappeared. Not a window of a few hours, not a guess based on grainy ATM camera footage, but the exact instant they went missing: 12:01 a.m. On. The. Dot. And that's because every student at the Freedom School in York, Pennsylvania, has a subcutaneous implant that tracks their movement on campus and monitors their biometrics. It's called a CHIP, for Campus Health and Individual Protection.

Somehow, both Nicky's CHIP and their phone stopped sending signals at the exact same moment.

JASPER BURKHART: That's just not supposed to happen. It would be really hard to sync something like that up.

OGDEN LAKE: The voice you're hearing is that of Detective Jasper Burkhart of the York County

Police Department, who is in charge of Nicky's case.

JASPER BURKHART: If someone wanted to disable Nicky's CHIP, they would have had to know about it in the first place.

OGDEN LAKE: I asked him if it was possible Nicky's personal identification tracker had been removed prior to their disappearance.

JASPER BURKHART: Not impossible, but unlikely. The CHIP was transmitting their vital signs right up until the last moment. Their heart rate was eighty-six beats per minute, much higher than normal.

OGDEN LAKE: Like they were afraid or stressed?

JASPER BURKHART: No. More like they were excited.

OGDEN LAKE: In the school's database, there are records of Nicky's vital signs from the last month. By cross-referencing them with S0ci@1 posts and campus surveillance, we can see that they're consistent with other moments when they were excited about something. When they were *happy*. Like watching a VR thriller with Simon or pulling off a skateboarding trick on the student-built half-pipe behind the school's tennis court. They were something of a daredevil. This could have been one of those daring moments. Except that whatever happened to them, it caused them to fall off the grid completely.

Is Nicky Montana alive? I hope so. Kidnapped? Possibly. Or maybe they simply decided to run away and start a new life somewhere else.

SCHUYLER MONTANA: Nicky wouldn't run away.

OGDEN LAKE: This is Nicky's father, Schuyler.

SCHUYLER MONTANA: I have a lot of questions, but their mother and I know that much with certainty.

OGDEN LAKE: Norah Montana agrees.

NORAH MONTANA: Never in a million years would they leave like that. Nicky was happy at the Freedom School. Something happened to them. Please help bring Nicky home.

OGDEN LAKE: Of course, it can be hard for families to accept that their loved one would do the unthinkable. This is Detective Burkhart again:

JASPER BURKHART: Anything's possible, of course. We know that Nicky and Simon were up to something, had been working on some sort of science project that was potentially dangerous. We just don't know if it went horribly wrong or if it all went according to plan.

OGDEN LAKE: In the next hour, we will share the facts to date. On our website, you'll have access to all the information the *Inexplicable* team has collected. As always, we protect and verify all of our sources to the best of our ability.

Anything could shed light on what happened to Nicky. And we're counting on you to notice the things we've missed.

Thank you for joining us. Stay tuned.

« « » »

**Audio released by court order from the
Freedom School, York, Pennsylvania,
and Avalon Wireless Technology, Inc.**

September 10, 2033, 2:30 p.m. ET,
Shyamalan Auditorium, the Freedom School

SIMON SHIN: Um. Is this the drama club meeting?

NICKY MONTANA: You're looking at it. And the

way you just projected, you're definitely in the right place.

SIMON: Thanks. Is it over already?

NICKY: You're the only one who came. I thought this was going to have to be a one-person show, and I was trying to figure out how to make more of me. I'm Nicky Montana. They/them.

SIMON: I'm Simon Shin. He/him.

NICKY: I know. I've seen you around. You're the new kid.

SIMON: I've been here almost a month!

NICKY: Still new, compared to the rest of us. I've been here since I was eleven. Still figuring out if I like it.

SIMON: If you haven't figured it out by now, when will you know?

NICKY: Probably not until ten years after I graduate. How are you enjoying Freedom so far?

SIMON: It's a little *too* free? No formal

classes, studying whatever you want, whenever you want . . . It's an interesting idea, but I miss my old school. At least I knew what was expected there.

NICKY: I've never been to a "normal" school, but they sound awful. Someone telling you what to do and where to go all day long. Having to study boring subjects and do homework and spend time with people you don't even like.

SIMON: It's not like that. Not exactly. How do you learn anything here?

NICKY: You get interested in something, and then you look for more information. The teachers can help you develop a self-study plan or run guided lessons. And there's at least one thing the Freedom School has that your old school doesn't.

SIMON: Oh yeah?

NICKY: Me!

SIMON: True. Until you figure out how to make more of you. Then every school can have one. Are you really that big a selling point?

NICKY: Well, I'm in the campus brochure. They used an old picture of me in the centerfold. Get your mind out of the gutter! It's just the collage in the middle of the magazine, but I like making it sound scandalous because it embarrasses them.

SIMON: Who's "them"?

NICKY: The people in charge. I bet they're listening to our conversation right now. Hi, Deepak! He's the IT guy.

SIMON: I've met him. They're really recording us?

NICKY: You didn't know? They're archiving every word we're saying right now. Video, too, probably. You've seen the cameras. There are also cameras you don't see. But all of them see *you*.

SIMON: Uh-huh. Um, is that legal?

NICKY: It is if you're here. Your parents signed the school contract, which means they signed all your personal rights away. You know what they say: "Privacy is the cost of Freedom."

SIMON: Who says that?

NICKY: You know. *[inaudible]*

SIMON: Well, it's been nice meeting you, Nicky Montana.

NICKY: Wait! Please stay. I didn't think anyone would actually show up, but here you are. I'm surprised you noticed my flyer. Maybe we can find a good two-hander to perform—that's what they call plays for two characters. You *can* act, right?

SIMON: . . .

NICKY: Me neither. This is going to be fantastic! And we're guaranteed a captive audience of at least one. Right, Deepak?

《 《 》 》

The Freedom School Security Footage:

Camera #NRTC19: Sector 84

2034.05.18-21:47:00

OFFICER #001138 LOG SUMMARY: The subject paces in front of the structure, talking into his phone, gesturing wildly. He stops and looks directly at the camera. Then he points his phone at the camera and continues to talk. He turns the phone back to himself and continues pacing. He seems agitated. It starts to rain.

« « » »

Excerpt from SimonSez Channel on GLiTCH.tv, livestreamed on May 18, 2034, 9:48 p.m. ET. Transcript annotated with AI-generated video description.

I'm actually glad they're getting all this on video. When the court orders them to release it, they won't be able to pretend none of this ever happened. Hear that, Deepak?

[It is raining heavily. The teen is drenched, pacing back and forth. Each time the teen turns, the cabin appears briefly in the background.]

It's really coming down now, huh? It's almost showtime. Security will probably send campus police to intercept me soon. They take curfew very seriously. And since I was suspended and sent home, I'm not even supposed to be on campus at all. But I had to come.

I've had a lot of time to think over the

last six months, and I've been wondering what would have happened if Nicky and I hadn't met. Would they still be here?

I'm sure that in some alternate reality, the two of us never became friends. If you believe in a multiverse of infinite possibilities, then there's a world out there resulting from every choice you make.

I know. That's a big *if*, and it hurts my brain whenever I think too hard about that "many worlds" stuff. As if one isn't enough to handle.

[Thunder rumbles in the distance.]

Nicky—my Nicky—is fascinated by weird theories and pseudoscience. Bizarre stories you'd find in the tabloids in the supermarket checkout line or on dusty shelves in the school library. Reincarnation. Alien autopsies. Bigfoots. Bigfeet?

Parallel universes.

When they started reading about that last one, they realized it was the perfect theory, because if it's true, it could be a scientific explanation behind all kinds of other stuff: ghosts, past lives, even Sasquatch.

They really want Sasquatch to be real. Maybe that's why they couldn't let it go.

Anyway, I wanted to join the drama club here because Dad had never let me do it before. I had always thought it would be cool to be in a movie or start my own GLiTCH channel, and pretending to be someone else for a while sounded kind of nice.

But according to my father, "Those silly activities are a waste of your time, Simon. You are a smart boy! Learn something to build a career on. Become a doctor or an electrical engineer." So, yeah, acting wasn't on the table.

But then he sent me to the Freedom School because he heard it was the best place for bright kids to excel. And maybe there's something to that. When you can commit yourself to your passion and learn at your own pace instead of sitting in a classroom of forty kids, being taught to pass a standardized test, you can do anything.

[The teen stops and places their hand on the door of the cabin.]

Anything. My passion wasn't engineering, but it certainly comes in handy once in a while.

I'd already been at the school for a month, on my own, without Dad watching my every move and judging me, but I still didn't have any friends. So I thought I should join a club to make some. And then I found Nicky's flyer—and then I found Nicky.

I can't believe I almost left that first meeting! But I'm used to fading into crowds, and when Nicky was the only one in the auditorium . . . I'm not good at one-on-one interactions. Something made me stay, though, and I'm glad I did. Even after everything that happened. That's still happening.

I know I'm better off for knowing Nicky. Even back home, I didn't have many friends IRL. I preferred hanging out with people on GLiTCH. I hoped that joining a club would help me get better at socializing in person. I thought forcing myself to get up on a stage in front of people would make me better at public speaking. And, well, here I am. I never could have done this stream before—or done anything remotely close to breaking a school rule.

Nicky's passions kind of became my passions. They gave me some direction and the courage to become the person I'd always wanted to be instead of who my dad and my teachers wanted me to be. The only expectation Nicky has is that you be your true self.

I'm sorry.

[The teen wipes their eyes.]

The weird thing is, I'm not sure Nicky's life would have changed all that much if we hadn't become friends. If I hadn't shown up for the drama club, Nicky totally would have put on a one-person show or found some other thing to be excited about instead of the Cage. As far as I know, that held their interest longer than any of their other projects the entire time they were at the school . . . aside from me.

Wow. I just realized I was probably another project for them. Did they put all that time and effort into the Cage because they wanted to or because I was into it? We're going to have a long talk when I find them. I've missed our long talks.

Nicky may not have changed because of me, but I do know one thing: they wouldn't be missing right now if I hadn't opened my stupid mouth.

≪ ≪ ≫ ≫

Inexplicable Podcast, Episode 41:
"Where Is Nicky?"
Published on the TrueCrime Podcast Network
on April 1, 2034
{transcript}

OGDEN LAKE: We can't speak to Nicky, of course, and Simon won't say what happened, so we talked to a few people who might have an idea of what was going on in their lives. "Brian" is a faculty member at the Freedom School who agreed to speak to us only if we used a pseudonym and altered his voice.

BRIAN: Nicky and Simon are good kids. All the kids here are. We select them as much as they select us. The Freedom School is one of the best democratic boarding schools in the area. Kids who come here can do anything they want—study anything they want or just play all day. They—

Right, this isn't an ad for the school. I just want you to understand the mindset we cultivate here. We like to say, "Your imagination is the limit, so the possibilities are endless."

Nicky's been with us for seven years. Simon . . . he enrolled last fall and had trouble adjusting. Some kids struggle when they move into an environment without structure, without anyone guiding their instruction. I know he had concerns about getting into a good college. No formal classes means no grades, of course, so he felt like he needed to work extra hard to prove himself.

I think his father pushed him toward the Freedom School, and Simon hates to disappoint anyone. He worries about his father, and I think perhaps this is one of those situations where two people each want what's best for the other, but that means neither of them ends up happy. Does that make sense?

Perhaps that's why Simon and Nicky hit it off so well. Simon liked having someone to tell him what to do. That probably sounds bad. It's not that Nicky is bossy, but they have a way of influencing others, pulling them along on whatever wild idea they have. And Simon . . . he isn't all that motivated, unless he has a specific goal in mind.

He's a planner—that's what I mean. Everything he did at the school, he was wondering if it would look good on a college application. Nicky wanted to know a lot about *everything*. Exactly the kind of student who thrives with us. They were always finding something new that would absorb them for days or sometimes weeks.

Yes, that's what happened with the . . . that's right, "the Cage." That's what they called it. Odd name for a study cabin, which is how it was originally pitched to the school board, which comprises students as well as faculty, by the way. They got approval to build it on campus, but they had to get the materials themselves and earn the funds to pay for everything. And it had to be available to everyone. We approve most student requests as long as they are safe. We had no reason to suspect it wouldn't be.

It was a big project, and some of the other kids joined in at first, but it was always Nicky and Simon's clubhouse, and consequently no one but them really used it much after it was built. Some kids said they got a weird vibe from it, and they didn't like hanging out there because it was in a dead zone.

Sorry, poor choice of words. Their cell phones couldn't find a network there, and they couldn't log into the school's Wi-Fi. You know how everyone is these days—we're online all the time. I don't know what would interfere with the signals like that, but the place may as well have been haunted. And yes, there were rumors about that, too.

OGDEN LAKE: The environment inside the Cage was even more unusual than anyone on campus was aware. A look at the data supplied to us from various sources shows that whenever someone entered the ten-by-ten-foot structure, constructed out of spare lumber, plywood, and corrugated sheet metal, they dropped off the grid. That's right—CHIPs even stopped broadcasting their biometrics and their locations.

Just like the night Nicky disappeared.

From studying Nicky's recent online search history, we know that this isn't supernatural at all. In fact, it couldn't be more scientific. But before I explain, one more note from our faculty representative:

BRIAN: Students are prohibited from removing or modifying their CHIPs, but we couldn't find any proof that they had. They followed all the school rules except one: students are not allowed in the forest after nightfall without permission and an accompanying faculty member, for their own safety.

OGDEN LAKE: Security cameras show Simon and Nicky entering the woods at 10:04 p.m. on November 15, just as a heavy thunderstorm was moving into the area. At 12:15 a.m., Simon stumbled out of the trees alone, drenched with rain. He stopped long enough to stare up at the security camera, tears streaming down his face. He glanced over his shoulder as if looking for someone. He flipped off the camera before getting on his bike and riding away.

≪ ≪ ≫ ≫

Nicky Montana's online search queries,
anonymously posted and verified

"Axel, are you recording everything I say?".
IP address 2010:db8::78e9:5555,
Room 1408, Lewis Hall, the Freedom School
Device ID: Axel Virtual Assistant App,
Avalon Speaker

"Axel, will you go [redacted] yourself?"
IP address 2010:db8::78e9:5555,
Room 1408, Lewis Hall, the Freedom School
Device ID: Axel Virtual Assistant App,
Avalon Speaker

"block listening devices"
IP address 2010:db8::78e9:3a0d,
Room 1408, Lewis Hall, the Freedom School
Device ID: Nicky Montana's personal computer

"legal school camera surveillance"
IP address 2010:db8::78fc:871f,
Shyamalan Auditorium, the Freedom School
Device ID: school-issued tablet

"turn off webcam"
IP address 2010:db8::78fc:871f,
Shyamalan Auditorium, the Freedom School
Device ID: school-issued tablet

"how PIDs work"

> *IP address 2010:db8::6612:b88e,*
> *cafeteria, the Freedom School*
> *Device ID: school-issued tablet*

"block chip + RFID"

> *Avalon Wireless network, the Freedom School*
> *Device ID: Nicky Montana's Android phone,*
> *OS Neapolitan*

"how to build a faraday cage + DIY + cheap"

> *IP address 2010:db8::4414:1a33,*
> *Suite 47, Matsumoto Hall, the Freedom School*
> *Device ID: Simon Shin's personal computer*

"scrap metal + local + free"

> *IP address 2010:db8::4414:1a33,*
> *Suite 47, Matsumoto Hall, the Freedom School*
> *Device ID: Simon Shin's personal computer*

« « » »

Audio released by court order from Avalon Wireless Technology, Inc.

September 15, 2033, 6:20 p.m. ET
IP address 2010:db8::78e9:5555,
Room 1408, Lewis Hall, the Freedom School

Device ID: Axel Virtual Assistant App, Avalon
Speaker

NICKY MONTANA: I am not being paranoid. That thing is listening all the time. Watch. Axel?

AXEL: Standing by.

NICKY: See? It's standing by.

SIMON SHIN: Isn't that what it's supposed to do? Stand by in case you need anything?

AXEL: I didn't get that.

NICKY: There are so many articles about these recording things they aren't supposed to, people being able to listen in on conversations.

SIMON: It has to be listening all the time so it can respond when you say "Axel."

AXEL: Standing by.

SIMON: Yeah, I know.

AXEL: I didn't get that.

NICKY: Listening, but not *recording*. I guarantee you this conversation is going to end up in an archive somewhere.

SIMON: And probably deleted. No one will ever read it. Even if you're right—

NICKY: I'm right.

SIMON: Even *though* you're right, there's way too much data for humans to review everything.

NICKY: That's what the algorithms are for. They listen for keywords, and then they flag them for human eyes. What are you looking for?

SIMON: Your tinfoil hat.

NICKY: Why would I have a hat made out of tinfoil?

SIMON: To shield your brain from electromagnetic fields, prevent mind control, etc.

NICKY: That's bonkers.

SIMON: That's kind of the point. Never mind. Anyway, your roommate, Axel, is very creepy. That's why—

AXEL: You really think I'm creepy?

SIMON: *That's* why I don't have one. That's why my dad doesn't have one. Why do *you* have one if you don't want to be recorded?

NICKY: I'm studying it. Looking for its weaknesses. It has no power over me if I'm wise to what it's doing. If you don't want an Axel, why aren't you—

AXEL: Standing by.

NICKY: Why aren't you more concerned about the Freedom School monitoring us with everything else? Phones, laptops, tablets. Security cameras. The things in our arms?

AXEL: "The Freedom School does not monitor or record student conversations or activities. These capabilities may only be accessed in an emergency that threatens the well-being of a student. Absolutely no information is recorded or archived, nor will it ever be. That is contrary to the very principles on which this school was founded."

SIMON: . . .

NICKY: . . .

SIMON: Axel, who told you to say that? Where did you get that information?

AXEL: Official statement from Headmaster Ayesha Washington, January 12, 2031, in response to *Montana v. the Freedom School*. Cosigned by student governing board and faculty.

NICKY: And it's *still* bullshit. I'm gonna turn off Axel.

AXEL: Standing—

« « » »

Audio released by court order from
Avalon Wireless Technology, Inc.

September 15, 2033, 6:22 p.m. ET
IP address 2010:db8::78e9:4224,
Room 1408, Lewis Hall, the Freedom School
Device ID: Simon Shin's Android phone,
OS Neapolitan

NICKY: Anyway, we can't talk about this freely anywhere on campus, obviously. Which means we can't talk about that other thing, either.

SIMON: What other thing?

NICKY: I told you, we can't talk about it. So I haven't mentioned it yet. I wish there was somewhere we could talk privately without being monitored or overheard. What's that look on your face? It's scary, but also kind of exciting.

SIMON: I have an idea. Remember that tinfoil hat?

NICKY: I am not wearing a tinfoil hat. I do not look good in hats.

SIMON: Same idea, but different. Bigger. Have you ever heard of a Faraday cage?

NICKY: Like what go-go dancers dance in?

SIMON: No.

NICKY: Is it the name of the cage thing where wrestlers have cage fights?

SIMON: No. It's like . . . a box that can block electromagnetic radiation. I built a small one at my old school for a science fair.

NICKY: How big can you make one?

SIMON: As big as you want, if you have the materials for it. And possibly a power supply. I'd have to look into it.

NICKY: Let's do that.

SIMON: We're just talking theoretically, right?

NICKY: Yes, in theory.

SIMON: I think I know why you keep Axel around now. You like the idea of someone who *has* to listen to you 24/7. You're holding him prisoner. Maybe I should free him.

NICKY: Shush, you. I'm trying to free all of us.

SIMON: I will not be silenced!

NICKY: That's the spirit.

≪ ≪ ≫ ≫

Video on Nicky Montana's S0ci@1 page
[blocked by the Freedom School,
recovered from archives],
October 22, 2033, 1:13 p.m. ET.

Transcript annotated with AI-generated video description.

[Teen 1 looks elated. Cheeks flushed, eyes bright. Their brown hair is braided into two pigtails, and they're wearing a T-shirt for the band the Eels and a pair of frayed stonewashed jeans.]

Simon and I did it! We finished the Cage today, and it is perfect. Take a look!

[They point the camera away from them and pan around the windowless room. It has four wood walls with a tin roof and a dirt floor. Copper mesh stretches over each wall. The camera ends on Teen 2, with messy black hair and a red hoodie, holding a hammer.]

I can't even post this live because *there's no signal.* This is awesome!

It's a little ironic that you're recording this for your S0ci@1 page, considering . . .

[Teen 2 spreads their hands.]

I'm just proud of this. We made this! Us! Together! And this is only the first step. Now we have a place where we can talk and plan without anyone listening in, unless we want them to.

[Teen 1 turns the camera back toward themself, and their expression gets serious.]

I know you're watching me, but I'm choosing to upload this. Don't ever forget that. It's my choice. And remember this, too.

[They squint into the camera and bring it closer to their eyes.]

We're also watching *you*.

« « » »

Inexplicable **Podcast, Episode 41:**
"Where Is Nicky?"
Published on the TrueCrime Podcast Network
on April 1, 2034
{transcript}

OGDEN LAKE: Nicky and Simon spent a lot of time in their homemade Faraday cage. I spoke to dozens of their fellow students, and there was plenty of conjecture about what exactly they were doing in there all the time. Classmates nicknamed it "the Love Shack." But despite the salacious rumors, no one really thought the two friends were romantically involved.

JORDAN MCINTYRE: They studied in there. They read books, played music. They just wanted a quiet place to themselves.

OGDEN LAKE: Jordan McIntyre is one of their few schoolmates who spent some time in the Cage, though anyone could have used it whenever they wanted, as it was built on school property. It was "too weird" for Jordan to want to go back. He describes what he saw firsthand:

JORDAN MCINTYRE: Nicky was always tinkering with something. They spent days covering every inch of the walls in aluminum foil, of all things.

OGDEN LAKE: Jordan shows me pictures of the inside of the Cage, which corroborate his story. While the supposed study cabin had been bare-bones at the beginning, only weeks later it was filled with electronics: speakers, cameras, microphones, all hooked up to a laptop.

Why go to all the trouble of creating a space where you couldn't be monitored or recorded by your smart devices, then fill it with recording equipment of your own?

JORDAN MCINTYRE: When I asked about it, they told me they were thinking of starting a podcast.

OGDEN LAKE: Another student, whom we're calling "Sarah" to protect her identity, claims that Nicky said they were filming a short play.

SARAH: I asked if I could participate, and they said I was already in it. What does that even mean?

« « » »

York Public Library Patron Record
#0182237988—Montana, Nicky.
Posted anonymously.

October 12, 2033
Fun with Electricity! Kids, Try This at Home, Miller, A.

Little Houses for Little Architects, Ali, S.

Surveillance State: How We Gave Up Privacy for Convenience, Barrow, C.

Heavy Metal, Clarke, M.

November 1, 2033

Hidden Worlds, Rex, H.

Parallel YOUniverses, Madison, X.

Same Earth, Different Dimension, Sloan, T., and Kelley, M.

The Lives and Times of Hugh Everett III, Everett, E.

November 11, 2033

Lightning in a Bottle, Browning, Z. [OVERDUE]

Quantum Immortality, Sheridan, B. [OVERDUE]

« « » »

**Audio released by court order from
Avalon Wireless Technology, Inc.**

November 7, 2033, 1:05 p.m. ET
IP address 2010:db8::78e9:5555,
Room 1408, Lewis Hall, the Freedom School
Device ID: Axel Virtual Assistant App,
Avalon Speaker

SIMON: It still hurts!

NICKY: Oh, stop. Don't be so theatrical. It's all in your imagination.

SIMON: Well, it definitely tingled. We used too much power.

NICKY: Or not enough.

SIMON: What are you doing?

NICKY: I'm making sure this is my dorm room. Did I make my bed this morning?

SIMON: If you did, that would be a first. Even I would be suspicious of . . . what, exactly?

NICKY: That we crossed over. We have to keep trying at different times of day. Maybe there's a moment when the barrier is more permeable . . .

SIMON: Nicky. This is disturbing. You're getting carried away. I don't want to do this anymore.

NICKY: We can't stop now.

SIMON: Where is all this coming from? You're suddenly so hung up on the existence of parallel universes. You've been reading and watching so much science fiction, you're starting to sound like a bad movie.

NICKY: No need to be mean.

SIMON: Just . . . I want to understand. Why does this matter so much to you? You have a wonderful life.

NICKY: My life's fine. It's this world that's messed up. There has to be a better one.

SIMON: Then let's make it ourselves.

NICKY: This is going to work. We just need more power. We have to be ready. If we do it right, we can break through.

SIMON: What could possibly go wrong?

NICKY: If you're afraid, you can just document it. But I can't do this without you.

SIMON: Give me one good reason why we should try this.

NICKY: Because we can.

SIMON: I knew I should have changed schools.

NICKY: Maybe you just did. Did I leave that book open on my desk?

SIMON: You're just trying to prove your hypothesis. If this is real, shouldn't we tell someone?

NICKY: No! Don't you dare. Don't even think about it.

SIMON: You worried they won't believe us?

NICKY: I'm more worried that they will. This is ours. This is happening to *us*, right now. I don't know why, and I don't want anyone to take the discovery away from us. Or try to stop us. I've never felt special before, like I'll actually do something important with my life. Have you?

SIMON: I'm working on it.

NICKY: Exactly.

« « » »

Inexplicable Podcast, Episode 41:
"Where Is Nicky?"
Published on the TrueCrime Podcast Network

on April 1, 2034
{transcript}

OGDEN LAKE: Did Nicky really believe that they had built a portal to a parallel universe? Or did they inadvertently build a death trap? Consider this conversation with Simon, recorded on his phone, only days before Nicky disappeared.

SIMON SHIN: Lightning? Sounds dangerous and stupid.

NICKY MONTANA: Look at it this way: if you get shocked and survive, then you're in one of the realities where you didn't die. Boom! Quantum immortality.

SIMON SHIN: Except that suggests there's a reality, or likely many realities, where you *do* die. I'm not a lucky person, and I don't like those odds. Especially if I'm in a universe where *you* don't survive.

NICKY MONTANA: That's sweet. But believe me, I'm not trying to kill myself. The lightning is just to generate enough power to create a stable passage so we can cross to the universe next door.

SIMON SHIN: It still seems risky.

NICKY MONTANA: The worst-case scenario is that we zap the Cage with 1.21 gigawatts and nothing happens.

SIMON SHIN: No, the worst-case scenario is that something *does* happen. Even if parallel universes exist and it's possible to visit them, what makes you think the one we'll end up in is any better than this one?

NICKY MONTANA: I just need to do something that matters for once.

OGDEN LAKE: So there you have it. Nicky knew there was a chance they would be hurt or killed that night, but it seemed worth it in order to prove the existence of another world—and leave this one. In that case, what does that make Simon? A survivor or an accomplice?

《 《 》 》

Weather report, November 15, 2033

Thunderstorm warning is in effect from seven p.m. until midnight. High winds, heavy rain. Flash flood warning, up to ten inches of rainfall expected. Lightning is a major threat. Stay indoors.

« « » »

Recovered clip from Nicky Montana's audio journal, recorded November 11, 2033. Micro-recorder confiscated from the Cage, 99 percent of data scrambled.

. . . figured it out. If there are . . . worlds touching ours, each of those might have their own Cage. So if two Nickys in two universes switch on the power at exactly the same time, that might be enough to connect . . . called quantum entanglement. Simon thinks I'm . . . but I'm worried about *him*. I don't know if we can generate enough power for both of us to cross, and whichever universe I end up in, I want him to be there. My Simon, not another one. Even if they're basically . . . same. Am I really going to do this? Of course . . .

« « » »

Excerpt from SimonSez Channel on GLiTCH.tv, livestreamed on May 18, 2034, 9:51 p.m. ET. Transcript annotated with AI-generated video description.

If I hadn't suggested the Faraday cage, Nicky never would have become obsessed with the idea. They said they wanted to prove we could do it, see what another world is like. But I think they loved the idea of finding a parallel Earth on which we didn't all live under society's microscope. It got to them after a while: the constant surveillance, always feeling like you're being watched, seeking attention and approval from strangers.

Just look at what happened after they disappeared. Ogden Lake calls me every day to try to get me on his podcast. He and his entitled fans have been digging into every last detail of our lives without caring whether they have the right or if it's the right thing to do.

I didn't really think it would work; that's the only reason I helped Nicky build that lightning rod and hook it up to the Cage. I almost didn't believe it when they disappeared—literally in a flash. So I don't expect you to believe me, but it's the truth.

Best guess: there's something about that area—maybe the barrier between universes is thinner there, somehow. Or maybe it's the Cage itself. If there are infinite worlds and as many Simons and Nickys, and enough of them built a Cage on the same spot we did, and they all powered them up at the same time . . .

We didn't build a Faraday cage. We built ourselves a giant Schrödinger's box. Google it.

The lightning strike was powerful enough to send Nicky over to another universe all on their own. They're there, I know it. I've snuck back into this forest before, and I can feel their presence. Like a ghost, but they're alive, just . . . on the other side.

[The teen reaches out like they're grasping for someone's hand. Lightning flashes, instantly followed by the sound of thunder.]

I wish I'd gone with them.

I've never felt like I fit in anywhere. One place seemed as good, or as bad, as another. But even within a multiverse, there's still only one Nicky. My best friend. And I know now that that's where I fit—in whatever universe they're in.

If our theories are right, I have to repeat the experiment to open that portal from this side at exactly the right moment. If I'm lucky enough, lightning will strike a second time.

[Voices shout in the distance over the pounding rain. The teen opens the door to the cabin.]

You might not even notice I'm gone.

[The teen steps across the threshold and closes the door.]

[End transmission]

[Show top comments]

COMMENT #13: Did you notice how his voice trembled at the end there? That was a nice touch! *eye roll*

COMMENT #14: i thought he was being sincere

COMMENT #16: He said it himself, he's being dramatic.

COMMENT #25: I think he's hiding something.

COMMENT #26: I don't think he's hiding anything anymore.

COMMENT #43: What a loser!

COMMENT #59: Anyone else think this sounds like a confession? I'm calling it: he killed Nicky and buried them under the cage.

COMMENT #60: How would that even work?

COMMENT #77: Anyone else think Nicky was superhot?

COMMENT #86: The cage is the key to this whole thing.

COMMENT #87: ^^^ Hard agree.

COMMENT #99: Not wanting to be under surveillance all the time isn't a crime. It should be our right. A basic freedom. It used to be.

« « » »

Police and Dispatch Recording,
May 21, 2034, 12:01 a.m.

Unit closest to the Freedom School, please respond. Reports of a fire in the North Campus woods. Fire department is en route. Two teens discovered on scene: missing persons Nicky Montana and Simon Shin.

« « » »

Inexplicable Podcast, Episode 41.5:
Follow-up to "Where Is Nicky?"

Published on the TrueCrime Podcast Network
on May 25, 2034
{transcript}

OGDEN LAKE: I was fooled. We all were. The disappearance of Nicky Montana, and the subsequent disappearance of their best friend, Simon Shin, on May 18, 2034, was an elaborate hoax.

After months of our collective research and analysis and theorizing . . . Nicky is back home. Conveniently, they reappeared right after Simon Shin's livestream went viral. And Simon, too, is alive and well after stepping into the Cage and vanishing in front of multiple witnesses as it was struck by lightning. Again.

Of course, I'm happy that no one was hurt. Their families are overjoyed. It's possible Nicky and Simon will face charges for perpetrating this whole charade, as well as for arson, though the official police report ruled the fire of May 21 an "electrical accident." Some eyewitnesses claim the Cage was struck by lightning a third time and burned to the ground. Fortunately, the fire was contained, and the Cage—which Nicky and Simon built themselves, remember—was set to be demolished anyway.

And while the two of them haven't explained

where Nicky has been for the past six months, they both claim they were only trying to get people thinking about how much of our lives is out there in public. How much access people have to us, even our most private thoughts, fears, and hopes. The Freedom School is now under investigation for recording student conversations without permission in violation of the wiretap laws in Pennsylvania. So, mission accomplished, kids?

Nicky and Simon also say they wanted to show how easy it is for the media to manipulate the truth and how easy it is to manipulate the media. The dramatic production they released— in which we have all unwittingly participated— rivals Orson Welles's *War of the Worlds*, which was famously so convincing that it sparked a nationwide panic in 1938. Perhaps it was a way to get Nicky's point across while furthering Simon's acting aspirations?

In looking back on all we've learned since our last episode and all the clues our listeners unearthed and pieced together from home, I believe some of the comments in our forum were in fact posted by Simon or Nicky, guiding the narrative into an outlandish fantasy. We will be scrutinizing those conversations and our processes carefully to prevent this type of abuse from happening again.

And yet . . . some things still don't quite add up. The night of Simon's livestream, at the exact moment he disappeared, Nicky's cell phone and CHIP signals briefly reappeared on the grid. They lit up in at least a dozen different locations at once before disappearing again, along with Simon's.

That shouldn't be possible.

I've continued digging, and I've found another intriguing fact: a CHIP can't be forged. They are unique to each student, functioning essentially as a digital fingerprint. Nicky's and Simon's CHIPs now have different fingerprints than they did before their disappearance. Again, we don't have an explanation. Only more mysteries.

Including this final one: an anonymous contributor sent me a photo this morning of a box-shaped structure under construction in an abandoned lot three miles north of the Freedom School. There are no city or private development plans on record, and the lot is owned by an anonymous investor. Could someone be building a new Cage? If so, this one is going to be much bigger.

Stay tuned.

SMILE RIVER

A.S. KING

Rose begat Grace and Grace begat Rose and Rose begat Grace and Grace begat Rose and Rose begat Grace and Grace begat Rose. And you will be the Rose who sets us all free.

YEAR 2051 / ROSE

The year is 2051. I am eighteen and my grandmother is eighty-one and she is telling me stories of when telephones were connected to walls with bouncy cords and how she only had three television channels, and she tells me she had her own face and her own mind and she could feel whatever way she wanted to.

"We used to get to places with big paper maps and then ask strangers for directions."

"No!" I say.

"They weren't even smiling," she adds.

"That's dangerous!" I say.

"You said that last time, too," she says, but we've never talked about it before.

Her nurses contain her in her room. Like solitary confinement, but with better food and larger bills. When she used to be allowed in the common rooms and the dining area, she would upset the others with her stories from the old times.

"It's because they remember." Her voice is a wing-clipped bird.

They won't even let her crochet.

"Did you really talk to people who didn't smile?" I ask.

"Smiling was supposed to be for when people were happy," she says.

"But unhappy people can hurt you!"

"There's a gray area," she says.

"I don't know what that means," I say.

"I know," she says, and cries into her hands.

"Can I drive to it?" I ask. "Do they hide things from the past there? In the gray area?"

She sobs.

"Do you want to take a drive with me?" It comes out singsong.

"I can't look at you!" she says.

The nurse knocks and comes in at the same time. She asks me to leave and gives me her biggest smile. She asks me to never come back. So many teeth. She tells me that the bill is overdue. She tells me that Gram needs to be fixed. The last thing I say to Gram: "I will find the gray area, and I will paint a picture of it for you!"

ONE YEAR EARLIER /
YEAR 2050 / ROSE

It is Friday and we are at the dinner table. Four of us. Me, my mother, my father, and Gram Rose. It's always the same. Every Friday. The only thing that changes is my father's excuse to leave the table early.

"I left my project notes at the office," he says.

No matter what excuse he uses, we allow it. The dinner table is better without him. We all have things to do tonight anyway. I have to prepare for tomorrow's regional competition. Gram Rose has to get back to crocheting a hat. My mother has to find a safe place to cry. I am seventeen.

All Roses in my family are secret weapons. I am a secret weapon. I will win tomorrow. All Roses in my family are fortune tellers. I am a fortune teller. I will win tomorrow.

The world record for holding a smile is still only five hours. It was set by a woman named Susan Homer, a resident of Altoona, Pennsylvania, who beat my old record by five minutes. She told a radio host after last year's Grand Champion Big Smile event, "It actually made me happier. Did you know that? Did you know smiling can make you happier? They've done studies."

She wasn't lying. They have done studies. But smiling doesn't actually make you happier. It only fools your brain for a little while so you forget about reality.

I go outside and look at the moon. People have told me many times that they can see a woman there smiling and I can see the woman's face, but she looks to me like she's crying. I'm not sure if that's some kind of sign.

My Gram Rose—I'm named after her—passed down to me the ability to live a paradox. I am happy-seeming all the time to fully meet community expectations, but under my manufactured smile, I have real thoughts and feelings, which, in 2050, is morally prohibited. This doesn't drive me to disappearance, as it has so many other girls and women. It makes me stronger / secret weapon. It fills me with hope / fortune teller.

I will shatter Susan Homer's record tomorrow. It's my last shot at the Big Smile, because my father is about to patent his new procedure. After this, TheBigSmile® will mean something else.

2100 / ROSE

You are in the center of the fourth-grade classroom at your school. You don't know what's going to happen today. You don't even know why you're here. You've been brought in—from your carpeted kindergarten room—so they can do experiments on you.

They are ten and eleven years old.

You are five.

You are not scared—this is routine.

"How are you feeling?" a kid with freckles and brown hair says.

You answer, "Happy."

They lock you in the dark supply closet for what feels like five minutes, then open the door.

"How are you feeling?" a kid with a scar on his chin asks.

You answer, "Happy."

Fifty fourth-grade kids smile. Congruently. Simultaneously. They smile like fifty clowns or fifty piano teachers. You smile in reply because you have already been taught that smiling is the only way out.

You have a gram named Rose—same name as you—and she tells you stories about a time when there used to be competitions for smiling and how she used to win them and how you are a secret weapon and how you are a fortune teller. She tells you that you can resist becoming like your mother. You don't know what she means. You are confused, mostly. All the time.

2150 / ROSE

You will be a miracle baby because your parents have decided a girl is worth the trouble. The boys in your preschool class will laugh at you and say you are dumb and ugly. One time, you will have your tiny arm broken when a boy pushes you off the playground equipment. He will mean to do it. You will smile as they set your arm in space-age plaster. Your parents will send you to a different school. They will have moved back from EPIC, the first moon settlement of its kind, so you could get a good Earth education. They will want the best for you.

You will get TheBigSmile® when you are five years old,

as required. Your face and feelings will be controlled from a network tower two miles away. You will not think to blow up the tower—not until high school.

You will want to go to college and be a scientist. You will want to stop the world from being swallowed by the rising seas. You will want to help the climate refugees find higher ground and food. You will want so many things, but you will not know what to do with the feeling of want, which is technically prohibited.

You will stare at the moon through your bedroom window and try to see the happy woman on it, because people have told you she is there. You will not be able to see the woman at all.

2050 / ROSE

Gram Rose is crocheting me a special hat. Her hands shake now, more than usual. My father says she's probably going to die soon. He says it, and my mother and I have to smile when we hear it, even though it makes me want to push him down the steps and kick him until he bleeds from his ears.

The house is quiet except for my mother's music and Gram telling me about how great I am before tomorrow's Big Smile. Behind the chair she's sitting in, there's a framed embroidery my mother made. IT COULD BE WORSE!

"You're a special one," Gram says. "You see through all this nonsense."

"Yeah," I say, but I don't know what nonsense she means.

"So much nonsense," she says.

"Yeah."

"I know what comes next," she says. "Do you?"

I don't want to pretend, so I don't answer. Gram Rose says she could see the 2034 Civil War coming—the closing of the borders, the restrictions, and the disappearing. "It wasn't that hard to guess what was coming," she says. "When they wrote the Family Solution Bill, I laughed!"

The Family Solution Bill is not funny. None of the three postwar Great Solutions are funny.

1. The Family Solution—All women* are subject to regulation by the state. "Because they are usually the problem." The state requires all women to smile at all times and feel nothing other than happiness. "Being happy is easy," the president said. "Just change your mind." (*Gender is assigned at birth.)

2. The Great Forgetting—All personal photograph albums, diaries, journals, and any other form of recording the past from before the Civil War are prohibited. "Burn them in neighborhood bonfires!" the president said. The Great Forgetting was a risk. Not every family would comply, and the government knew it.

3. The New Feel—All mental healthcare is canceled. "Each of us is as damaged as the other, and there is no room in this new America for accommodating

anyone's *feelings*," the president said. Therapists and psychiatrists moved to other jobs. Medication went black market until it ran out. Smiling competitions were invented as a way to keep everyone on board.

I competed in my first Big Smile at age seven. My father got me a trainer—a man named Alonso. My mother was against competitive smiling. She and Gram Rose barely endured it. I thought then that they were jealous because my father told me they were jealous. "Neither of them has a smile like yours," he would say. I liked him doting on me—every girl likes a doting father.

I won my first Big Smile in March of 2045. I was twelve. My father bought me three fresh chocolate eclairs at the local bakery, and my mother was made to watch me eat them while my father told her how crooked her smile was and how she couldn't make a cake that wasn't dry and a bunch of other things I can't remember now. Tears raced down her cheeks, over the upturned edges of her lips, and onto the walnut dining table.

I won every Big Smile after that for years, setting record after record. But then Susan Homer from Altoona, Pennsylvania, showed up at regionals and started winning. After too many losses, I became my father's lab rat. I have a first-generation chip, same as my mother had, which allows me no control over my smile. It's always there, no matter how I feel. Plastic surgery for upturned lips and popped cheeks has been around since the end of the twentieth century, but what my father does is different. He puts implants in the brain. No one should have trusted him with this technology.

"You can see it, right?" Gram says. "You can see the nonsense."

"Yes, Gram. I can see it," I say.

I see myself grinning in the antique oval mirror on the living room wall. I miss looking trustworthy. I can tell Gram misses it, too.

2100 / ROSE

You are in the hospital drive-through checkup lane in the back seat of your mother's car. Your mother is listening to a happy song on the radio and singing along. You are six.

When she pulls up to the area where the nurses are, the nurse uses a scanner to check your mother's cranial neural electrodes and the batteries in her chest unit.

"Everything looks great," the nurse says.

"Excellent!" Mom answers.

"How do you feel?" the nurse asks.

"Great!" Mom says.

"You look great, too." The nurse is used to looking at people like your mother and saying they look great. She says it a hundred times a day. Her smile is iridescent.

The nurse turns to you. "And how are you, little Rose?"

You smile and say, "I'm happy."

The nurse gives you a lollipop. She says, "Only one more year for you!"

You wonder if other six-year-old girls dread the surgery like you do. You are very young, but you can sense that something about it is wrong. It seems unnatural to be happy all the time, even though that's all adults seem to want from you since you can remember. You make a pact with yourself to memorize what it feels like to be afraid of the dark.

2150 / ROSE

You will take walks with your mother around the neighborhood. She will point to the nearby river and tell you, as she has many times, that they didn't have rivers on EPIC. "No rivers, no blue sky, and no birds. Dismal place to bring up children."

She will point to the river and say, "That is where to find me when it's over." She will say it in such melody. She will perform it—her smile stretched wider than her hips. "That is where I'll be."

You will be six years old. In ten years, you will understand what this means. But at six, you will feel a different kind of happy when she says it. You will feel like a fortune teller.

2050 / ROSE

My mother is still singing to music in the kitchen, and it sounds like she's baking. Gram and I speak in whispers as she crochets and I stretch my face and neck for tomorrow's competition.

"My father is having an affair," I say.

"With Nell Cruz," Gram says. Nell Cruz is my father's work partner at his lab.

"He kissed her on the lips right in front of me one time when I was younger," I say.

"That must have been confusing."

"He told me that's how people say goodbye where she's from," I answer.

"Bahamas," Gram says.

The Bahamas are underwater now.

"I just wish he wouldn't lie about it so much. How many times can he leave project notes at the office?" I say.

"He's a monster," she says. "Look at what he did to you."

The surgery happened at the end of summer. My father didn't want to lose me, he said, so he only used a first-generation implant. And he didn't tell anyone, not even my mother, so no one noticed. Except Gram, the minute she saw me. She didn't gasp or zing out or anything like that. She just hugged me and said, "You are worth more than you think."

School this year has been a lot easier. The other girls in my classes have to concentrate so hard to smile all the time, they miss whole lessons. Twice last week, girls were removed from exam classes because they let themselves concentrate on the questions rather than on their faces. I don't have to do that anymore.

"People should pay you just to stand near them," my father says. He says it with his signature frown. Men are still allowed to have those. Men are allowed to have everything. Like always.

Mom enters the living room. "I made cookies!"

Gram says, "That's nice, Grace. What kind?"

"Chocolate chip!"

I get up and move toward the stairs and say, "I'm going to do my homework."

"Well, at least take some cookies while they're still warm!" she says, and happy-jogs back to the kitchen to put some on a plate for me.

I go upstairs and write down all my feelings. It's not my homework, but it helps. I write two poems—one about being sad and one about being scared—and I save them even though they could get me arrested. Gram Rose says I'm a good poet. She should know. She's an artist herself. She knits special hats with aluminum foil inside them so the government can't control the wearer's brain. She says they're a joke, but deep down, you can see how she hopes the hats will work.

I love her weekend visits from the nursing home. Usually she talks about the time before the Civil War or what things were like when she was growing up.

"We used paper maps to get places—big folding things," she'd say, arms stretched wide to show me how big, "and when we got into town, we'd have to stop and ask someone for directions to the specific place we wanted to go."

"How did you find people to ask?"

"People were out and doing things," she'd say. "Not like now. People were more active then. It was so different."

All Grams say this. Grams since the beginning of time have said this.

"Sometimes I'd even walk right up to a person who wasn't smiling and ask them how to get to wherever your grandpop and I wanted to go."

"That's so dangerous!"

"We were real rebels," she would say, laughing.

Gram would get quiet then. I would always think she was hiding something. My mother would confirm it. She and Gram had a secret. It was in the attic—my mother's favorite place to cry. I was not allowed to go there, but that didn't mean I didn't go there.

2100 / ROSE

You have concentrated on your fear of the dark so much, and you are so afraid of it, you scream-cry when your father turns the light off at bedtime. You are sent to a doctor. The doctor says you are malfunctioning / hysterical. You are six and a half years old.

"She'll be fine once she's worked on," the doctor says to your father. "Until then, make her sit in the dark as often as you can."

On the drive home, your father tells you that he has prepurchased a condominium in a future moon settlement. "We'll live there one day, and you'll be happy then," he says. He does not understand that you already live on a moon. He does not understand that all girls live on a moon, or some other cold planet that makes no sense.

When you get home, you are locked in your mother's

dark walk-in closet until dinner. Your father says, "Doctor's orders," as he blocks the door from the outside with a chair.

In your rage, you throw yourself into the corner of the dark closet and discover a secret panel. It leads to a small attic with a battery-powered light. In the attic is a box with old items in it. One of the items is a photo album with pictures of people from the old times. A lot of them look like you.

2150 / ROSE

You will compete in your first Prettiest Smile competition at age seven. You will win a silver medal and twenty thousand dollars that will pay off your family's surgery debt. You will not seem at all like the descendent of a murderer / the man responsible for the disappearance of everything good.

There will be a difference now between just smiling, like every other female in the last hundred years, and pretty smiling. Pretty smiling will be an art form like ballet or mastering the cello. There will be training and preparation involved. Dedication and tenacity.

You will do your face exercises daily. Roll your neck. Tone your cheeks to the shape of crabapples. You will apply tooth whitener with a brush and make sure it doesn't touch your gums or lips. If it does, it will burn them. You will be so scared of the pain that your bottom lip will quiver even though you don't know what fear is.

When you're done, you will feel relief. That's all. Just relief.

Your parents will be overjoyed.

Your parents will always be overjoyed.

2050 / ROSE

When I drive Gram back to the nursing home, it's always her last chance to say all the things she can't say. We are the perfect team for this. I have many things I can't say, too.

"Your father may be the miracle man or whatever they call him, but he sure is cheap!" She laughs when she says this. "He asked if there was a way to get a cheaper dinner menu. I told Grace—it's a nursing home, not a fucking restaurant!"

"Fuck!" I say.

Swearing with my grandmother is completely illegal, which is why we do it only in the car while we drive the long way back to the nursing facility—over the mountain, where there's the least chance anyone will overhear us.

"Well, screw him, anyway," I say. "He doesn't even care about us."

"That fucker has done nothing but destroy this whole family."

"He's about to destroy the whole world," I say. "Everyone will look like me and Mom soon."

"Not me. Not fucking me," Gram says. "So help me god, I will throw myself into the big river."

I get paranoid when she says this. It is the most illegal of all things, capitulation.

"What are you going to do when he comes for your brain?" Gram asks. "Because you know he's going to do that."

"Not if I keep pretending."

"Rose. Honey. I don't mean to condescend, but that fucker is coming for your brain. Trust me. Look at your mother."

I reach up and touch the crochet work on my head. "The hat will save me."

"Dammit, girl!" She pounds the dashboard with her fist. "You can't be complacent!"

"I love seeing you angry," I say. "But seriously, I won't let him come for my brain, okay? I really won't."

"It's not going to be up to you," Gram says. "Remember the night they took my Grace away."

Four months ago, when a pregnant Nell Cruz showed up at the front door of our house, my mother went crazy. She threw a lamp. She screamed. She ripped her own hair out of her scalp. All of this while she smiled wide with her first-generation chip—same as mine.

"We're going to help you," Nell said to my mother. "It's going to be okay."

My father looked at me as he dragged my grinning, furious mother through the open front door and into Nell's car. "She needs an operation."

Gram Rose took me into her little guest bedroom adjacent to the kitchen. We looked out the window and saw my mother slumped on my father's shoulder in the back seat.

When my mother came home three days later, she

couldn't stop singing songs and dancing. She took up needle-point. She needlepointed slogans.

THE BRIGHT SIDE IS THE BEST SIDE! THINK HAPPY THOUGHTS! SILVER LININGS ARE EVERYWHERE. LOOK HARDER!

By the time we're approaching the nursing home, Gram has gotten out so many curse words and angry growls, and she even cries a little and says aloud the names of the people and times she misses. Most of all, she says, she misses the Bahamas.

"Beautiful place," she says. "I'm so sad you'll never get to see it."

She tells me to check the attic. She says there's a map there.

"Of the Bahamas?" I ask.

She says, "It's more than a map. You'll see."

When we pull into the circular driveway where I can drop her off, we are both smiling, and our minds are free from negative thoughts. Ideal female citizens.

The nurse scans Gram to make sure she's not carrying any weird germs, and Gram says to me, "Good luck tomorrow! I know you'll win this time!"

The nurse says, "Good luck, Rose!"

2100 / ROSE

You are a month away from your surgery date, and even though you maintain your smile for everyone else, you know you can be yourself with your grandmother. She comes to babysit in the hour between when the school bus drops you off and the time your mother comes home from her job.

"How are you today?" she asks.

You whisper, "Sad and scared."

Your Gram Rose, once the holder of the world record for smiling—twelve hours, which was the maximum amount of time the competition would go and which stopped all Big Smile competitions going forward—says she wrote two poems that she will read to you one day when you are older. She wears an old crocheted hat she says has tinfoil in it. She says it's okay to be afraid. "It's okay to not feel like they say you should."

You say, "I feel like no one wants me here."

She says, "You are so precious. We all want you here."

"Not the real me," you answer.

"I do. I want the real you," she says.

When you start to cry, she lifts you onto her lap and says three things over and over into your hair as she rocks you. "You are a secret weapon. You are a fortune teller."

You want to tell her that you don't feel like either thing. You feel like a balloon without a string. You are still so afraid of the dark, you cannot even bear to look at pictures of the moon. You are scared to move there one day. You do not feel like a secret weapon. You do not feel like a fortune teller.

She says, "You are worth more than you know."

2150 / ROSE

In your attic, there will live hidden things that nobody but you knows about. A paper map with symbols drawn on it. A book of old photos. A book of old poems. A journal that has been in your family for seven generations—started by a Rose who was born in 1970 and liked to crochet.

In the journal, you will learn everything the government is hiding from you.

In the journal, you will learn everything the government has done to you.

In the journal, you will meet three other women from your family named Rose who, like you, had mothers named Grace.

In the journal, there will be an epigraph. *Rose begat Grace and Grace begat Rose and Rose begat Grace and Grace begat Rose and Rose begat Grace and Grace begat Rose. And you will be the Rose who sets us all free.*

You are the Rose who will set everyone free. You will focus all of your energy, aside from your Prettiest Smile training, on what you will have to do to achieve this. You will be thirteen years old when you start making your plan. You will write the first two steps in the journal.

Go into science. Stop the monsters.

Today, early and before the competition, my father and I stop at the lab together. I haven't seen Nell since the night she came to take my mother four months ago.

"Wow!" I say. "You're really pregnant now!"

Nell smiles and says, "These things happen!" and gives an animated shrug.

My father says to me, "Keep yourself busy. I won't be long."

He and Nell disappear into their secret lab, where paraplegics walk and unhappy people smile. Miracle man. An hour later, on our trip down in the elevator, my father says, "You are the best thing that ever came from your mother."

I let a moment run by. Before the elevator doors open, I say, "Maybe if you were home more, you'd see how great she is."

He slaps me roughly, across my cheek.

I smile the whole time and think about how great my mother is. She's funny and happy and all the things she's supposed to be.

My mother's smile could stop time because she *means* it. From her heart. She is that happy. The problem with this is, my mother has depression. She is every bit as sad under that smile as Nell is pregnant under her lab coat and my father is a liar under that skin.

———

2100 / ROSE

You are on a cold metal gurney and there are lights in the ceiling. You know what's going to happen today. They are going to drill tiny holes into your skull and make you happy forever. Your parents have paid for TheBigSmile® 2XL package, which includes both emotional and physical augmentation. This one can even wipe away ugly memories, so you've protected yours by writing them down in your mother's secret attic journal. Your first-grade handwriting looks so silly next to the other entries, but you feel less confused now.

The surgery will be fast, but the new-generation implants take a few weeks to integrate and heal all the way. You've been educated about proper hygiene and how to slowly get used to the change in sensation in your cheeks and around your mouth. You are seven years old.

They shave part of your head. They attach you to machines. The last thing you hear is someone asking you to think about a puppy counting backward from ten.

When you wake up, your parents are there and two hospital people, too.

"How do you feel?" they ask.

"Happy," you answer, still groggy.

They smile. Congruently. Simultaneously. They smile like four clowns or four piano teachers.

You only ever wanted to be yourself. You liked yourself.

———

2150 / ROSE

You will write your college application essay on Nell Cruz, a groundbreaking Bahamian biomedical researcher from the twenty-first century. In order to get into college, you must praise her science and her years devoted to WalkAgain® and TheBigSmile®.

The real reason you will be interested in Nell Cruz will be her personal story—how she raised two children by herself after her lover, your great-great-great-grandfather, went missing, how she tried to reverse TheBigSmile® trend, and how she started the underground implant-removal service that is lovingly known, in quiet circles of rebels, as TheBigFinger®.

You will be sixteen. Your college applications will go unacknowledged. Your mother will tell you it's your own fault for not writing about a reasonable topic—she will tell you Nell Cruz was a nobody. You will argue amicably, and she will win by saying, "Find me her obituary!"

You will know that Nell Cruz did not have an obituary.

No women after the Civil War got obituaries.

It made the disappearing easier.

2050 / ROSE

The lighting feels hotter than it has before. I'm on the competition stage with five other finalists, including Susan Homer. Her smile is just so fake. I mean, all our smiles are fake, but hers is annoyingly fake.

I roll my neck a lot and roll my shoulders forward and then backward. I forget my father's slap in the elevator. Today I don't care about tilting my head or where my shoulders are or any of the things I used to care about. I am an endurance machine. I could be thinking the worst thoughts and still win this thing.

By the sixth hour, I'm the only one left. Susan Homer has ice packs on her face in the green room, and little Portia Jones's mom is performing compression massage on her cheeks. She smile-screams that the cramps feel like fire.

My father left hours ago.

Before the competition started, I asked him, "How long should I go after they drop out?"

"Use up all twelve hours," he said.

"That's totally suspicious, though."

"Let them suspect!" he said.

My mother is the one who shows up for the medal ceremony. Most of the other audience members have left. Even second-place Susan Homer is gone.

"I'm so proud of you!" my mother says as we pack up my competition gear—water with straw, catheter with bag of piss, leftover snacks and snack wrappers. "You could have done twelve more, too, if they'd have let you."

And that's the thing. With these chips in us, my mother and I are smile-competing every minute of the day and winning. Gram will love to hear about how I probably killed smiling competitions, either way. She always said it was all bullshit.

On the drive home, I follow the moon as the car navigates the road. I can see the woman. She is no longer crying. She is grimacing, as if someone has done something disgusting in front of her. I feel like I am the one who did something disgusting in front of her.

2100 / ROSE

You are so relieved to be alive. Every day, you wake up with this joy, and it is so exciting, you run down the steps and jump into your father's arms.

"Look at how pretty you are!" he says.

Your mother's smile, a standard TheBigSmile® model, will look more and more like a wince. She still makes the best cinnamon toast in the world.

She says, "Today they will evacuate Miami."

Your father says, "All those people with nowhere to go."

"It's so sad," you say.

They stop chewing and look at you.

"I mean, it would be sad if I could feel that, but I can't," you say.

They look as if they don't trust you.

"In ten or twenty years, we'll live on the moon anyway," your father says. "Stable climate, good view, and a great place to raise my grandchildren, right, Rose?"

You don't think about whether or not you like yourself anymore. You don't think of anything at all except the things you learn in school. Your Gram Rose, grand champion of smiling competitions, still comes over every day for an hour, and the two of you play a game of checkers. You haven't told her yet that you found the journal.

You remember having a sort of bond with her. Something special.

You feel something about it—like gravity.

You are eight years old.

2150 / ROSE

You will be inside your boyfriend's home health pod, and you will be naked. You will be seventeen, in love, and anyone who looks at you will think that you are still augmented, but they will be wrong.

The smile is from the love.

The smile is from the freedom.

You will cry only in the shower, where it makes sense.

Underage sex will be encouraged, because underage marriage will be encouraged / life is short / your friends are disappearing. You will feel like a liar because you will have no intention of marrying this boy. You will just like the smell of his scalp and the feel of his shoulders and the way he tells you he loves you.

You will know he is lying. Rose from 1970 will have already written that down in the journal hidden in the attic.

He doesn't love you. He has no ability to love you. You will have to love yourself.

That's what it will say.

You will read it as often as you can so you are never fooled.

The next week, your boyfriend will accuse you of having feelings. He will make a scene at a train station. He will yell. He will slap you across the face. You will smile through it all. He will push you backward until you fall over, and the onlooking commuters will smile congruently and simultaneously—like three hundred clowns or three hundred piano teachers—as you fall to the concrete.

When you wake up, you will be in a hospital, and you will not feel anything but happy. You will not know to feel sad about it, either.

A month later, you will find out that you are pregnant.

A month later, you will wander the alleys of South Philadelphia, asking where to find the doctor. It will be all you know how to say, and you won't even know why you're there, but eventually, you will be escorted into a small basement room.

Two women will treat you. They will know precisely where to make the incisions.

"We couldn't get the smiling one out, but hopefully you can feel now," they will say when it's over. TheBigFinger® / Nell Cruz is part of you.

You will instantly want to cry. You will put your hand on your belly. You will feel real joy. And then relief. And then dread. It's harder this way, but worth it.

You will go home, and your mother will hand you a letter from a college.

You will say, "I'm pregnant."

She will say, "Congratulations!"

You will open the envelope and read an acceptance letter. You will burst into tears. Your mother will call the police. Before the call can connect, you will hit her over the head with the nearest object—an heirloom lamp.

Your mother will be okay. The lamp will break in its weak spots. There will be a note hidden inside the base. It will say, *You can find me in the river with the other fish.* It will be signed *Grace* and dated 2050. It will occur to you that this was written by your great-great-great grandmother—the doctor's wife. Miracle man.

2050 / ROSE

I am seventeen. I have just set the last-ever world record in smiling. No one else knows that yet / I am a fortune teller. As we drive home, my mother says, "I got a call today. Your Gram isn't doing so well."

"She seemed fine last night when I dropped her off."

"Something about her moods," my mother says.

That's code. My mother is acting like she doesn't know the code. She takes a scenic route back to the house. She drives by the big river. She slows in places, making sure no one is behind her on the country road. She points.

"What do you think it's like?" she asks.

"It's February," I answer. "I'd say it's cold."

I don't want to think about the river. I don't want to

imagine all the bodies in it. Everyone knows about the river. No one talks about it, not even if they see someone walking in. It's just a thing to do now. I turn on the radio.

"Twelve hours!" a radio host says after a commercial break. "My cheeks would fall off!"

I turn off the radio. "So what are they going to do about Gram?" I ask.

"I don't know," she sings. "They can't find her at the moment. I hope she feels better very soon."

That's code, too.

When we get home, I stay in the car for five minutes, claiming I need some time alone, and I cry because I have disgusted the moon. I eventually go inside to find my mother baking more cookies and dancing around the kitchen with a wooden spoon. Gram Rose is standing quietly in the doorway to her old room. "You're here!" I say.

Gram says quietly from the doorway, "I'm not going back."

My mother chirps, "You will go back, and you will get fixed."

"I don't need to be fixed."

"You're unhappy, and I can't look at you!" my mother says.

"You used to be such a deep well of a person," Gram says to her. "What an imagination! The way you'd play your saxophone!"

"I never played a saxophone," my mother says.

"You married a monster. He ruined you," Gram says.

"He ruined all of us," I say.

My mother can't admit it to herself. Patient zero. The original Big Smile. I don't tell Gram about how she asked what the river is like today, because it's too hard to tell a mother that her daughter is going to die. Plus, Gram is a fortune teller, just like me. She already knows.

My father arrives home. Even on a competition Saturday, he works past ten. Gram Rose scurries off to hide.

I expect him to congratulate me and hug me like he used to. I look for eclairs or any sign of celebration. As he walks empty-handed toward the door, I realize that my father's slap this morning was a goodbye. I'd spoken my mind / it was over. I am a breathing advertisement, is all. Presales and hype.

He stands inside the door and speaks to my mother.

"I'm moving out. I plan to live with Nell and our son," he says.

"Did she have the baby?" I ask. He ignores me.

"I know you'll be happy here by yourself," he says.

My mother smiles and nods while she removes cookies from metal cookie sheets and places them on a wire cooling rack.

"I tried all I could to make you happy," he says. "I really did."

My mother doesn't say anything. Hums a tune. Taps her foot.

"Please, Grace," he says. "Say something."

My mother smiles and looks around the kitchen. She says, "I love you."

He says, "Don't be like that!"

She says, "I hope you are happy with Nell."

He says, "You have to complicate everything!"

She says, "I wish you the best of luck."

He swings at the nearest thing he can find—a vase of winter-bought supermarket flowers—and sends them flying across the room. He takes a step forward, cocks his arm back again. My mother juts her jaw out a bit to give him a good target while I rush to get between them. Next thing, Gram Rose is at the back door, aiming his own shotgun at him.

"I will kill you right here," she says. She is not smiling. Only my mother and I are smiling.

My father doesn't know what to say / how to smile / puts his hands up.

There is silence / cheap flowers all over the floor.

Calmly, my mother scolds, "Now, Gram Rose, put that dangerous thing down!" She turns back to my father with her most fluorescent smile and says, "Go on, dear one. Get your things and go where you are needed."

We eat cake and ice cream for dinner.

I read my mother's last entry in the attic journal later that evening. *Men have hard, cold hearts. Women have warm, soft ones. This is why the world is breaking. Men want our hearts. Men have always wanted our hearts. Men don't want our hearts. Men have never wanted our hearts.*

2100 / ROSE

You are still afraid of the dark. You don't know why. You don't tell anyone, because fear feels like an old friend. You are growing up now. You know what's expected of you. Yet you continue to refuse to look at pictures of the moon.

They still do experiments—today three high school boys follow you home, and they make you afraid of the obvious. Except they don't know you can feel afraid. Most girls just smile all the way through whatever the boys want to do to them. Your mother is waiting on the porch with her car keys and handbag. It is checkup day.

You are in the front seat now, and the nurse scans and checks both your and your mother's implants.

"Have you thought about upgrading?" the nurse asks your mother.

"No. I'm so happy now, I can't imagine changing it."

"The 2XL has a new model coming!" the nurse says.

"I don't even know how they could improve this," you say. "The 2XL is so great!"

The nurse laughs and laughs. She leans into your mother's open window. "I hear this new one makes everything you eat taste like chocolate!"

You ask, "What if you don't like chocolate?"

Your mother looks at you like she always has.

The nurse says, "Rose, can you step out of the car and come stand here for me?" She points to the circle drawn on the concrete.

While the nurse goes to get some special scanner or whatever, your mother says, "How can you not like chocolate?"

You are in her walk-in closet all over again. Nothing you ever feel or say is right. No one really wants you around—the real you.

You think about taking a walk by the river tomorrow. You think about this a lot now.

Even though you are afraid to look at it, you think maybe moving to the moon, cold and desolate as it is, might be the right thing to do. It might be the only thing that keeps you alive. Your father will get his grandchildren, and there will be no rivers.

2150 / ROSE

You will be a pregnant college student. Your chip will keep you smiling, and your brain will work out the rest of the plan. At thirteen, it was *go into science / stop the monsters.* At eighteen, in the top science program on Earth's East Coast, it's more like *destroy everything / rebuild the algorithm.* It will be as simple as replacing the instructions fed into women's brains. The instructions will be in the chips, updated through the network. You will know not to blow up network towers until you change the code. You will have to convince the others. There will be others.

"Think!" you will say. "We have to upload everything first." You will hack it. You will gain access to every code ever written by the Miracle Man / murderer. You will reverse engineer the data / decompile the source files. "Even if we all end up frowning, it will be worth it," you will say.

Your Gram Rose will tell you stories through the journal. How her family moved to the moon, how her father brought boys home for her to make his grandchildren, how she did what she was told but didn't really like boys. You will wish she hadn't disappeared—especially so young—but nobody knows how disappearances happen. If you stand by the river and watch the women float by, like underwater traffic on a busy rush-hour freeway back in gasoline days, all of them will have an unmistakable smile. No one pushed into it could smile like that.

You will hear that logic so many times, it will become yours.

No one pushed into it could smile like that.

The women you will save will be your biggest threats. When you change the algorithm, they will either wake up and resist or choose to keep smiling because men like them that way. They could turn on each other. You will not know what will happen until it happens.

You will know only that your punishment will probably be the river.

You will walk there after sunset one night after a microbiology exam. The moon will be full, and if you look at it long enough, you will see the settlement billboards, flashing casino neon. You still will not see a woman. You will stand with one hand on your belly, feeling the kicking of the next Grace, and your other hand over your mouth. You will not let them see your smile as they shuffle—dead, moonlit, lined like factory-canned sardines, smiling like a thousand clowns or a thousand piano teachers—down the riverbed to wherever they end up. You will write the best algorithm you can. You will save us all. If you end up in the river, you will know you did the best you could.

2050 / ROSE

The night my father murders my mother, we eat cake and ice cream for dinner. My mother lets loose her secret.

"I can do both, you know. Feel and not feel."

Gram Rose grunts.

I say, "I've been reading the journal. This is how it always was."

Gram Rose grunts again.

"I'm sorry about your father," my mother says to me.

"You don't have to apologize for him," Gram says. "Rose knew this was coming."

"I thought he'd at least congratulate me," I say.

"It's a big day," my mother says, "for both of us."

"For all of us!" Gram says.

"I'm going to take a walk," I say. They tell me how cold it is outside and not to go in the direction of the river. When I put on my crocheted hat, I feel like a fortune teller.

I see the future as I walk. I see my daughter and her daughter after that, and her daughter after that, and then her daughter, too. They smile at me, congruently, simultaneously, like cloned clowns and cloned piano teachers. It's like looking in a mirror that expands through time.

I point and tell each one what I see even though I don't know who they are and when they will live. I only know they will live.

"You will marry at seventeen."

"You will kill a man."

"You will go to college."

"You will disappear."

"You will write the algorithm."

"You will have a soft, warm heart."

"You will save us all. Rose 2150, you will save us all."

When I arrive at the river, I see my mother in her favorite dress and shoes. She is still holding the wooden spoon—sometimes women bring something that defines them. *No one pushed into it would bring a wooden spoon.* My father is standing behind her. Someone is standing behind him.

I turn around. I hide my smile under my scarf.

On my walk home, I see a stranger standing on his porch.

He isn't smiling, so I ask him for directions.

"That's dangerous!" he says to me.

The moon is bright in the night sky. I look up and see the woman there, and for the first time, she is smiling. It feels like instructions.

When I get home, the police are there for Gram Rose. They can't find her.

When I get home, the police are there for me. They can't find me, either.

We make a pact to follow the rules for a little while.

I get Gram back to the nursing home safely, and she puts on her smile and stops talking about the old times.

I hide our attic journals under the floorboards. I go buy a newspaper with me on the front page. I drive myself to the SmileClinic®. Fortune Teller. Secret Weapon.

This is how I will save us all.

CONTRIBUTORS

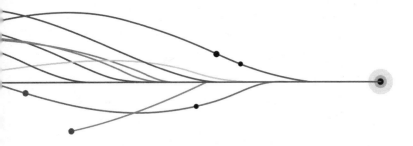

WILLIAM ALEXANDER is a National Book Award–winning Latinx author of unrealisms for young audiences. His novels include *Goblin Secrets*, *Ambassador*, and *A Properly Unhaunted Place*. He teaches in the Vermont College of Fine Arts program in Writing for Children and Young Adults.

Will says that "On the Tip of My Tongue" "started to accumulate the moment that I found out about Lagrange points and wondered what we might be able to build in such places—either on purpose or improvisationally. I also strive to write about disability, accommodations, and adaptive tech as expansive possibilities rather than symbols of loss and limitation."

K. ANCRUM is the author of the award-winning thriller *The Wicker King*, a lesbian romance called *The Weight of the Stars*, and the Peter Pan–inspired thriller *Darling*. K. is a Chicago native passionate about diversity and representation in young adult fiction. She currently writes most of her work in the lush gardens of the Art Institute of Chicago.

"I wrote 'Walk 153' about loneliness, cross-generational friendships, and technology being used to bring people closer to their environments," K. says. "Exploring the richness of the world through one-on-one travelers turns the YouTube-familiar GoPro experience into an intimate expression of care between the people who roam and the people who watch them."

ELIZABETH BEAR was born on the same day as Frodo and Bilbo Baggins, but in a different year. She is the Hugo, Sturgeon, Locus, and Astounding Award–winning author of around thirty novels and more than a hundred short stories. She lives in western Massachusetts with her husband, writer Scott Lynch.

Bear says the inspiration to write "Twin Strangers" arose from "thinking about how integral social media and the ways we present ourselves online have become to our self-images. We're so aware now of being on display all the time. In the future, we're going to need to find ways to navigate the demands of being online and available and 'seen' semi-constantly with our need for privacy and a strong self-identity. As who we are when nobody is looking becomes more elusive, it also becomes more important."

A. R. CAPETTA is an acclaimed and best-selling YA author of the strange, scientific, magical, mysterious, and queer, including the quantum physics–driven Entangled duet, *The Lost Coast*, *The Heartbreak Bakery*, *Echo After Echo*, the Brilliant Death duology, the *Stranger Things* novel *Rebel Robin*, and the best-selling Once & Future series, coauthored with their spouse, Cory McCarthy. For fun, they cowrote a paper with Dr. Julia J. C. Blau in the *Journal of Creative Writing Studies* on the perceptual science of storytelling, which is about as nerdy as it gets. A. R. Capetta teaches in the Writing for Children and Young Adults MFA program at Vermont College of Fine Arts.

A. R. writes: "I've always been drawn to the search for life in the cosmos—and the idea that it might be so much closer, and weirder, than people imagine. To connect with life that didn't originate on Earth, people will probably have to put aside a lot of assumptions and expectations. Which: good! Learning to decenter ourselves is key to many parts of existence, and I was fascinated to look at this on the species and planetary scales. Galileo discovered Jupiter's moons four hundred years ago, but the possibility of going to Europa in the near future is both new and very real. These ideas came together in a science-driven epistolary exchange between two humans, which leads to even bigger adventures of connection."

CHARLOTTE NICOLE DAVIS is the critically acclaimed author of the Good Luck Girls series and a graduate of the New School's Writing for Children MFA program. She currently lives in Brooklyn and loves comic book movies and books with maps in the front.

Charlotte was inspired to write "Cadence" because "as I grow into my own nonbinary gender identity, the one thing I've always wished I could change about myself has been my voice. Queer people often talk about 'gender envy'—I get that whenever I hear a voice that's the perfect combination of tenor and rasp. This got me thinking about a not-too-distant future where people could pick and choose customizations for themselves, almost like video game characters—which also got me thinking about some of the consequences of such technology."

NASUGRAQ RAINEY HOPSON is the author of the short story "The Cabin" in the award-winning collection *Rural Voices: 15 Authors Challenge Assumptions About Small-Town America*. She is a tribally enrolled Inupiaq, an illustrator, and an arctic gardener. She currently lives in Anaktuvuk Pass, Alaska.

Nasuġraq says she wrote "The Weight of a Name" after looking for Inuit-centered and Inuit-written science fiction and finding the results slim to none. "Science fiction has always been my first love, mainly because it contains so much hope," she says. "I found the world building in this short story to be incredibly rewarding mentally; to imagine our people in the future thriving and advancing was spiritually uplifting and healing."

A. S. KING is the author of more than a dozen novels that have garnered the Michael L. Printz Award, the *Los*

Angeles Times Book Prize, and many other honors. Her titles include *Switch, Dig, I Crawl Through It,* and *Please Ignore Vera Dietz.* She is a passionate advocate for teenagers and their mental health. She lives in Pennsylvania.

A.S. writes: "For fifty years, I have watched technology advance while humans stagnate in old patterns and ideas. In one hundred years, we will have permanent lunar bases, paralysis reversal, and an array of brain implants, but toxic masculinity's whims will still control women. 'Smile River' represents the conveyor belt of this history—the long line of women we've kept quiet with outdated bullshit."

E. C. MYERS won the Andre Norton Nebula Award for his first novel, *Fair Coin,* and is the author of the SOS Thriller series and the *RWBY* young adult books *After the Fall, Before the Dawn, Fairy Tales of Remnant,* and *Roman Holiday.* His short fiction has been published in various anthologies, including *Mother of Invention, A Thousand Beginnings and Endings, Hidden Youth,* and *Kaleidoscope.* He also writes for the serialized podcast *Orphan Black: The Next Chapter.*

About his story "The Cage," he says, "I'm fascinated by how our surveillance society is increasingly affecting people's lives and freedoms. The alarming prevalence of personal data online makes individuals vulnerable to harassment and exploitation, but it also holds everyone accountable for their beliefs and actions like never before. Meanwhile, social media empowers both 'armchair detectives' and law enforcement agencies to leverage this data—and even collaborate with each other—to expose hidden truths and bring criminals to justice. While potentially a powerful tool for positive change, surveillance and social media can be abused, like any technology, to manipulate audiences and shape new realities."

JUNAUDA PETRUS-NASAH is a writer, soul sweetener, runaway witch, and performance artist of Black Caribbean descent, born and working on unceded Dakota land in Minneapolis. Her work centers around wildness, queerness, Black diasporic futurism, ancestral healing, sweetness, shimmer, and liberation. Her first YA novel, *The Stars and the Blackness Between Them,* received a Coretta Scott King Honor. She is the cofounder with Erin Sharkey of Free Black Dirt, a Black experimental healing art collective. She is currently working on her second novel, *Black Circus*, set in the '90s, about a young Black woman studying circus.

Junauda says, "As a Black child growing up, I had to learn how to decolonize my psyche around the negative ideas about Blackness. This world has perfected the commodification of Black culture while simultaneously oppressing, degrading, and criminalizing Black people and their existence. While the impact of Black culture and labor is sacred and central to the US, there is an unspoken caste system and a history of erasure. In 'Melanitis,' I wanted to contemplate this tension and center the very juicy and yummy experience of being Black despite living in a culture that doesn't know how to love and honor us."

WADE ROUSH is a technology journalist and audio producer based in Cambridge, Massachusetts. He is the host of the podcast *Soonish*, about the technology choices we can make in the present to create a better future, and the author of the nonfiction MIT Press book *Extraterrestrials*, about the history and science behind the idea of life on other worlds. *Tasting Light* is his second foray into anthology work; he also edited the 2018 edition of *Twelve Tomorrows*, a long-running hard sci-fi anthology series copublished by the MIT Press and *MIT Technology Review* magazine.

"I learned so much from the brilliant authors we recruited for this book, especially my coeditor, A. R. Capetta," he says. "I think the writers have done exactly what we asked them to do—bewitch a new generation of young adult readers with hard science fiction—while also showing that there's so much room for stories about characters with a variety of under-represented backgrounds and identities. One of these days, I'm going to have to follow their example and write some of my own sci-fi!"

WENDY XU is an award-nominated illustrator and comics artist. She is the cocreator of *Mooncakes*, a young adult fantasy graphic novel published in 2019 by Lion Forge Comics/Oni Press. She lives in Brooklyn with her partner and cat.

Wendy says, "I was inspired to write 'The Memory of Soil' after interviewing biologist Merlin Sheldrake about his book on fungi, *Entangled Life*, and our discussion that ensued about using better metaphors to communicate scientific understanding. I had never considered the living world to be, well, alive. We are taught in school that organisms (especially the small, invisible ones) are, more or less, automated machines rather than living things in their own right. A robot, in theory, is also a machine ruled by nothing more than algorithms and subroutines. But the nutty thing is, we don't even know *how* certain artificial intelligences learn things. We humans make these machines, which in turn learn and grow, and we can't even fathom why. All of these concepts coalesced into the idea of a very human girl, who has been taught her whole life that she is just a cog in a social machine, and a robot who wants to be more than that."